The Salisbury Manuscript

A BLACK BAT MYSTERY

The
Salisbury
Manuscript

by
William M. Green

The Bobbs-Merrill Company, Inc.
Indianapolis / New York

c,/

S

Copyright © 1973 *by William M. Green*

ISBN 0-672-51855-4
Library of Congress catalog card number 73-3779

Designed by Sheila Lynch

Manufactured in the United States of America

First printing

BL FEB 4 74

For Hannah and Bob Green

The Salisbury Manuscript

A BLACK BAT MYSTERY

THE BANK VAULT was all stainless steel, white formica and shadowless fluorescent light. It was as still and sterile as a hospital, odorless and soundless, except for thc whir of the air circulating system and the whisper of rubber soles as the attendant shuttled back and forth between the huge walk-in safe and the small counting room.

Charles Ford and the courier from Havana stood on either side of the doorway to the counting room, watching as the attendant brought in the metal safe deposit boxes one by one. There were eight metal boxes altogether. Four belonged to Ford, and they were fully laden and extremely heavy. The attendant chose to use a dolly cart to move them from the safe to the counting room. Four belonged to the Cuban, and they were empty. The attendant stacked the boxes in two piles of four each on the formica-topped counting table. They came up almost to his shoulders. Then the attendant withdrew, leaving the two men in privacy.

The courier nodded, indicating that Charles Ford should proceed. Ford opened the first of his heavily laden boxes. He looked delighted as a child as his eyes swept across the ranks of little lead soldiers lined up fifteen abreast and thirty deep, filling the interior of the metal box. He stood back so the Cuban could view the toy parade.

The Cuban reached into the box, selected a lead soldier at random, studied it with admiration, weighed it in his palm and then set it down on the counting table.

He opened his locked diplomatic pouch and withdrew a pair of heavy shears. Then he cut the little lead soldier in half. There was a flash of gold in the white fluorescent room as the soldier's torso was divided from its legs. The Cuban nodded approvingly and set the two halves of the figure down, its exposed golden core glowing incandescently inside its lead veneer.

Together the two men emptied the full boxes and filled the empty ones, the Cuban selecting a lead soldier at random from each of the boxes and shearing it in half.

When all the soldiers had been transferred, the Cuban put the shears back into his bag and withdrew a sealed package. It was far less substantial in weight and volume than the gold, but it was equal to the gold in value. Charles Ford broke the seal, examined the contents, expressed his satisfaction, and resealed the package. Then he placed it carefully in one of the metal boxes belonging to him.

The two men shook hands and signaled for the attendant. The attendant could not help but notice how the weight of the boxes had changed. But he gave no sign. He was a model of Swiss discretion. The transaction was ended. The metal boxes packed with gold now belonged to Cuba and would reside in Cuba's niches in the vault's steel wall.

The courier could now go home and leave to his government the disposition of its newly acquired gold. For Ford a new ordeal was just beginning. He would have to meet his contact and arrange for the sale of the package. He would have to cross the continent to Holland without alerting his pursuers. But if they did sniff him out again, he had to insure that this treasure he had spent half a lifetime acquiring would not fall into the hands of enemies and strangers.

*** 2

IVES DARTED A LOOK up and down Minster Road before entering the red-lacquered phone booth. His caution was born of instinct more than necessity, since he was quite sure he wasn't being followed. He peeled off his gloves and sorted through a palmful of coins. He had the supple hands of a pianist, slender fingered, well manicured, strong. He was a slightly built man, with a face that might have been drawn by a child, all angles and circles, and all a little askew. It was a face without highlights or planes. The nose was a checkmark. The lips were a line. Steel-rimmed spectacles circled jade button eyes. A wisp of a mustache like tiny moth's wings seemed in danger of being inhaled. He was a harmless enough looking man, almost clownlike in appearance, especially since his nose and cheeks had been daubed apple red by the British cold. But his innocuous looks belied the wickedness of his calling and the expertise with which he practiced it. He was an inquisitor by trade, a specialist at extracting information from unwilling subjects.

He dialed the operator and placed his call. There was a buzzing and then a pickup at the other end of the line. Ives deposited his coins to complete the connection.

"Rawlings here," came the voice from London.

"He's gone to ground," said Ives without preamble, "in a cottage out on the Salisbury plain near old Sarum. Hasn't left the place in five days except to stand in the doorway for a breath of air. Has his groceries delivered—or did, until day before yesterday. Made an indecent proposition to the delivery boy. The kid's family own the store. They cut off deliveries but didn't call in the police. Don't want a public scandal. But half the town's talking about it already."

"Has he seen you?"

"Couldn't have. Not yet, anyway. We've been taking turns watching from behind good cover. Damned uncomfortable, but he hasn't seen us."

"And you're sure he hasn't moved?"

"Not unless he's made himself invisible."

There was a pause at the London end while Rawlings considered.

"Do you think he might have brought the goods in with him?"

"We're sure he didn't. You can't move gold about that easily. Of course, he might have had it stored there all along. But I doubt that. He sublet the cottage from a very respectable old couple. I think he must have left it somewhere on the Continent before we picked up his scent."

"Could they have been delivering it piecemeal with the daily groceries?"

"Not very probable. The store's an old family-run affair. Been in business in the same spot for generations. Mother, father, and two sons run it now. The younger son's the one who does the deliveries. Although, as I said, there haven't been any the past two days."

"And you're sure he hasn't slipped out on you?"

"We're sure."

"I think it's time to have a look. If he doesn't have it there with him, it's time to find out where he does have it. We've waited long enough."

*** 4

"I'll have the information for you within forty-eight hours." Ives welcomed the order to move. He and his partner were growing tired of watching and waiting.

"Handle him with care," Rawlings advised. "We don't want a corpse on our hands, not until we've found out what we need to know."

"Have you ever known me to let a subject go sour?"

"I'll be waiting to hear." The receiver clicked down in London, breaking the connection. Ives hung up his phone, drew on his gloves and left the phone booth.

CHARLES FORD slipped out from between frigid sheets. He sat for a moment on the edge of the high English bed hugging himself for warmth. His short legs dangled, his toes barely touching the floor. His soft, doughy belly rolled yeastily over his groin. His pudgy epicene features were drawn down in a pout. He had slept in his clothes, with a woolen sweater over his shirt and woolen socks on his feet, and still he was cold, cold as death. The feeble heaters in the room were no defense against it, nor would a fire have been had he the wood to build one in the hearth. The cold was radiating out from a core of ice inside him. He had not known a moment's comfort or warmth since Amsterdam nine days ago. The chill of the drizzle that misted over the canals had settled in his liver and crystallized there. There was a glacier forming inside him.

Had he been able, upon his arrival in England, to take a room with central heating at a good London hotel, he might have found some comfort. But necessity dictated that he go to ground in the countryside. The cottage he had leased between Sarum and Salisbury served his need for isolation but compounded his misery. It was an old cottage, and centuries of winter were stored within its walls. He didn't wonder that the owner sublet it every year and fled to the south of France from December through March.

Shuddering, he padded across the creaky oak floor, parted the curtains a crack and peered out through the small window. The manicured fields all around were dun colored with winter and crackling with frost. There was no wind; only a moist, frigid stillness, like the inside of a meat locker. In the early morning light he could see the slender Gothic spire of Salisbury Cathedral rising out of the gently rolling plain three or four miles away. Six hundred yards away, where the dirt track that led from the house joined the main road, he saw the parked Jaguar sedan. They had found him.

It had taken them six days. He hadn't thought it would take that long. Perhaps it hadn't. Perhaps they had been with him ever since he had stepped off the plane at Heathrow, dogging his tracks as they had done, to no avail, clear across the Continent.

He had given nothing away. But now he had come to the end of the line. The fact that they now showed themselves so openly told him so. It would not be pleasant, but it was inevitable. There is a limit to how far a man can run.

He wondered if they would be thugs . . . or pacific practitioners of their art. Would they advance on him with brass-knuckled fists or with needles loaded with sodium pentothal? In either case, he was certain they would not be coming with intent to kill; a dead man could tell them nothing. And in that knowledge lay his strength; in that and in the knowledge that Casey was due to arrive from the States in three days' time. Casey could be depended on to help him in this predicament. She could always be depended on.

*** 6

3 ***

CASEY FORD WAS ALONE when she was wakened by the ringing of the telephone. It was dark in her room and she couldn't see the clock. But she knew it must be sometime in the middle of the night. Let the damned thing ring itself out, she thought. She'd just barely dropped off to sleep, it seemed, and the day ahead was going to be a bitch. She buried her head under the pillow to shut out the sound.

The phone kept ringing. She gave up. She groaned and reached over and wrenched the receiver from its cradle.

"Is this Mrs. Ford?" a solicitous voice inquired.

"Whatever you're selling, I'm not interested." She slammed the receiver down and rolled over. The phone began to ring again. Casey wrenched the receiver up again.

"Whoever the hell you are," Casey said thickly, "you'd better have a damned good reason for calling. It's the middle of the night."

"It's eight-thirty in the morning, Mrs. Ford..." the smooth unflappable voice droned.

"Thanks, but I don't subscribe to a wake-up service. Who the hell are you?"

"I'm Mr. Walters... Department of State."

"Oh. Jesus! Don't tell me you woke me up to tell me there's something wrong with my passport."

"Not as far as I know, Mrs. Ford," the voice intoned with practiced patience. "Were you planning a trip abroad?"

"Tomorrow."

"Has someone already contacted you in this matter, Mrs. Ford?" The voice sounded puzzled, confused.

"I don't know what matter you're talking about, Mr. . . . What did you say your name was?"

"Walters. Of course not. I'm sorry."

"Of course not, what?"

"It was just that your mention of an impending trip abroad misled me into believing, for a moment, that perhaps you were involved in some way in the—ah—arrangements."

"What arrangements, Mr. Walters? This is a business trip."

"Yes, of course. You're in publishing, aren't you?"

"That's what it says on my passport application."

"Yes. That might explain the manuscript, too."

"Are you talking to yourself, Mr. Walters? Because if you're through talking to me, I'd like to try to get back to sleep."

"I'm sorry. I *was* thinking aloud." His voice became very businesslike now, almost mechanical. "You *are* Mrs. *Charles* Ford?"

Casey groaned. "Is that what this is all about? Is Charles in some kind of trouble again?"

"Is he often in trouble?" Mr. Walters inquired with interest.

Casey reacted protectively. It had become almost instinctive with her where Charles was concerned. "He *is* in the habit of overextending his credit," she said lightly. "Nothing a check or cablegram for a few hundred dollars won't cure."

"I see," Mr. Walters said almost ruefully. "May I ask when you last saw Mr. Ford?"

"About two years ago. On a trip overseas. May I ask what this is all about?"

*** **8**

"You were separated then?" he asked rhetorically.

"Years ago. That's on my passport application, too. Now, what seems to be the trouble?"

"Has he any other family that you know of?"

"Not that I know of, Mr. Walters," she said wearily. "I think they were all wiped out in the war."

"Then perhaps that might explain it."

"Explain what?"

"Well, you see, you are listed on his passport as next of kin."

Casey felt her heart begin to pound. She sat straight up in bed and flung her legs over the side. "Is Charles hurt, Mr. Walters?"

"It is my unhappy duty to inform you that he is dead, Mrs. Ford. If you will permit me to come by for a few minutes, there are certain things that might best be discussed in person."

4 ***

RAWLINGS GOT THE NEWS less directly, but just as joltingly, through a lurid news item on the second page of the *Mirror*. An associate named Fred Dorff brought it in.

"Something's gone wrong," he announced as he slapped the newspaper down onto Rawlings' desk. "Might have expected it," he added sullenly as he turned his back, trod heavily across the room, and dropped down into a leather lounge chair. The cushion sighed as it compressed under his weight. He was a big, hulking man with the neck and shoulders of a wrestler. His eyes were narrow slits in a concrete pillbox of a face. He restlessly combed his stubby fingers through his thinning dark hair while he waited for Rawlings to finish the newspaper story.

The alliterative headline read, "Two Bodies Suggest Sordid Crime of Passion on Salisbury Plain." To most other readers of the *Mirror* it was a titillating story laced with intimations of homosexuality and sadomasochism. To Rawlings it was evidence of disaster . . . and betrayal.

There was a photo of a stone fireplace and chimney rising eerily out of a pile of charred rubble on a hilltop. Beside the photo was a cutaway sketch of how the cottage had looked before the fire had razed it. There were arrows pointing to what had been the bedroom of the cottage, where the nude bodies had been found. Two males, fairly well cremated, their sex established by skeletal structure.

Police were able to ascertain by a signet ring on a bone of the little finger of the right hand that one of the bodies was Charles Ford, an American who had rented the cottage a week previously. His passport and personal papers were found in an aluminum traveling case in his hired car parked outside the cottage. The identity of his visitor remained unknown.

Rawlings got up from behind the desk, a lean, deceptively fragile looking tower of a man in a flawlessly cut double-breasted suit. His youthful, even-featured face was framed by creamy-smooth yellow-white hair. Finely etched lines radiated from around stoic steel-gray eyes. There was a grim set to his firm thin mouth. He folded the newspaper around the news item and tossed it back onto the desk. It landed with a smack. Dorff came and picked up the paper and scanned the story again.

Rawlings pivoted awkwardly and limped toward the window, swinging a stiff left leg from the hip. His kneecap had been smashed in a fight five years before.

"Was Ford queer?" Dorff asked.

"He might have swung both ways." Rawlings' voice was flat and cold. "But I don't see that it matters. They made all the wrong guesses out there. Ives knew they would and took advantage of it."

"You mean the business about the kid?"

"Maybe that's what gave him the idea he could get away with it. But we know for certain something the police out there can never know; that was no lover who visited Ford last night. It was Ives and Martin."

Rawlings turned away from the window, away from the bleak prospect of Hyde Park in the winter. A few more days of this cold weather and there'd be skaters on the Serpentine. "My only question is, which one of them is lying there with Ford and which one has cleared out with the information?"

"I'd bet on Martin; he's the muscle. I don't think Ives would have it in him to kill two men." Dorff said it disdainfully, as if the inability to kill were a handicap.

Rawlings' voice was as icy as the weather outside. "Consider the prize . . . and consider who he was killing. Ford was vermin. And Martin was a thug. Ives is a man of intellect with the capability for rationalization. Men of reputed character have killed and betrayed for less than the wealth the information he got from Ford will bring. Anyway . . . Martin wouldn't have had the brains to camouflage the crime. He'd have done it and run."

Dorff was simmering inside. He knew that Rawlings considered him closer to Martin than to Ives in intellect and capability. But he was loyal . . . and this was no time to show his resentment.

"What do we do now?"

"We find Ives," Rawlings replied flatly. "I wish this weren't such a private affair. It would be very convenient if we could bring the police in to help us."

"What if he gets to the gold before we find him?"

"Then we'll find him afterward. Nobody can hide forever. Ford learned that much."

"I'll get out to Salisbury and try to pick up his scent."

"Yes. Do that. And . . . if you find him . . . and find out what he knows . . . remember, nobody can hide forever."

"I'm no Ives," Dorff said resentfully.

"Ives was no Ives either . . . until yesterday."

*** **12**

5 ***

MR. WALTERS ARRIVED at Casey's apartment at nine
o'clock, barely thirty minutes after he had wakened her.
He was as trim and compact as an athlete, and as gray-
garbed, neat and solemn as a newly fledged banker. Slightly
puffy eyes in an otherwise clean-cut face indicated that he
might have been up for hours with this business before he
had actually placed his call to Casey.

Casey was still in her robe. But she'd brewed a pot of
coffee and she invited him to sit down and share some
breakfast with her in the living room. He sat down patiently
and studied her, nonplussed, as she brought in a cart with
a coffee pot on it, along with jam and bread and a toaster.
She plugged in the toaster behind the couch.

Casey began to pour the coffee but her hand was shaking.
Mr. Walters got up and took over, somewhat relieved to
see at least this manifestation of feeling. When the coffee
was poured and they were both seated again, he on the
couch and she on the edge of the easy chair, Mr. Walters
cleared his throat.

"First . . . may I express my deepest sympathy."

"Thank you, but you hardly need to. You didn't know
Charles and you don't know me."

"It's a matter of form, Mrs. Ford," he said reproachfully.
He was plainly bewildered. He knew how to deal with
hysterics . . . but equanimity threw him. "I take it then that

you and Mr. Ford had not separated on the best of terms."

"I was fonder of Charles than I should have been, Mr. Walters. It's just that it seemed to me inevitable that he should have ended this way."

"You are assuming his death was not of natural causes." She sighed. "I suppose I am."

"Why should you make such a supposition?" Was it an inquiry or an accusation?

Casey shrugged. "I just knew Charles, that's all."

"You're right, of course. You were aware then of his nefarious activities?"

"I suppose I was."

"May I ask what they were, as far as you know?"

"Does it matter?"

"It might."

"He gambled a great deal . . . and lost a great deal . . . and avoided paying his debts. He peddled worthless stock in a number of worthless corporations. I suppose somebody he bilked or somebody he welched on finally got impatient."

Mr. Walters made a pretense of sipping his coffee, but he was merely holding the cup to his lips, stalling while he tried to frame his next question. Finally he said, "Mrs. Ford, there is something I must ask you, of a most unsavory nature. But I must ask it."

Casey nodded, indicating that he should go ahead.

Mr. Walters coughed and cleared his throat unnecessarily. "In your knowledge of Mr. Ford . . . can you tell me . . . is it possible . . . that he might have carried on affairs of a homosexual nature?"

Casey threw him a guarded look. "Why do you ask?"

Mr. Walters coughed and cleared his throat again. "The British police have requested that we ask."

"The *British* police?"

*** **14**

"He was living in a rented cottage on the plain outside Salisbury when . . . it happened."

"Why do they want to know about his sex life?"

"Because as they reconstruct last night's events . . . Mr. Ford was visited by a male friend. Both bodies were found in what was left of the bedroom after the fire."

Casey's hand began to tremble again, rattling the cup against the saucer. She placed them both down on the coffee table. "You didn't tell me there was a fire."

"Yes, I'm afraid there was. Perhaps a candle knocked over. Perhaps a cigarette. Perhaps a spark from the shotgun blast. It was one of those thatched-roof cottages. They're virtual tinder boxes."

"A shotgun?" Casey began to turn pale.

"Would you like some smelling salts, Mrs. Ford? I carry a few ampules . . ."

Casey shook her head. "Who fired the shotgun?"

"Do you really want me to go on, Mrs. Ford?"

"I want to know what happened."

Mr. Walters sighed. "It would be difficult to say exactly, except for the condition of what remained of the skulls. The stock of the weapon was reduced to charcoal. Even the barrel was twisted from the intensity of the heat. I really don't think you want me to go on."

"I do."

Mr. Walters looked like he might wish to make use of one of his own ammonia capsules. But he continued. "If it's of any consolation to you, it would appear that Mr. Ford was not the perpetrator, but the victim. The condition of the skulls indicate that his visitor did the shooting. Mr. Ford took a blast full in the face from a distance of three or four feet. Then his visitor apparently placed the barrel in his own mouth."

15 *

"If this visitor was a lover, as you imply, why would he have come armed?"

"The gun was in the house. The owner, from whom Mr. Ford rented, is a sports enthusiast. There may have been a . . . quarrel. You know how those things can happen."

"So that's the end of it?" she asked numbly.

"I'm afraid so. The fire was burning beyond control before it was even sighted from the town. By the time aid arrived the place was a furnace. There was nothing left to do but pour water on to quicken the cooling of the ashes."

Casey sighed. "Thank you, Mr. Walters, for telling me."

"I judge you to be a very strong woman, Mrs. Ford . . ."

Casey nodded. There was a vacant look in her eyes. She was aware that Walters was speaking again, but she hadn't heard the words. She asked him to repeat what he had just said.

"I asked if, to your knowledge, Mr. Ford ever had literary ambitions."

Casey shrugged. "He had all kinds of ambitions. Most of them amounted to nothing." She smiled wryly. "Sure, he had literary ambitions, like everyone does who hears about a novel that made somebody a millionaire. That's really inspiring, you know, although it hardly ever happens. Every now and then when we'd meet and he'd get a snootful, he'd start rhapsodizing about what a wonderful book his life would make. I'd tell him that everyone's life would make a book if only they'd sit down and write it. I'd tell him that if he'd take the time to write it, I'd take the time to help him with it. It would certainly have been more constructive than whatever else he was doing."

"Did he?"

*** 16

"What?"

"Write it."

"No. He never did a lot of things he maybe should have done. And he did too many things he shouldn't have. He sent me a letter a few months ago. From Switzerland. Lugano. He said he had really latched onto a sensational idea for a novel. He even sent me the first page he'd written, just to show me he really meant it. He was going to write like a fiend and send me the chapters as he wrote them, and the next time I was in Europe we could talk about it."

"Did he send you the chapters?"

"No. I didn't expect he would. You have to understand Charles. If I were a building contractor instead of an editor, and he was feeling low, he'd have written telling me he'd just had a great idea for plastic houses and we'd have to talk about it next time we got together. He must have been sitting up there on an Alp freezing his ass off and down to his last nickel and he'd just read about some best-selling author who had just bought a villa on the Riviera. That was really all he ever wanted, you know . . . to be rich and play in the sunshine all day. That's why he gambled and conned and did all the other crummy things he did. He really thought there was a pot of gold waiting for him somewhere."

"It seems he did actually try to write that novel."

Casey looked up in surprise.

"There was a manuscript, of sorts, in a suitcase in Mr. Ford's hired car outside the house. The police opened it, of course."

"I'd like to see it, if I may."

"Of course. It's your right. The envelope it was in was addressed to you. We can request them to forward it here."

17 ***

"No. I'll be in England in a few days. I'd like to go to Salisbury. Perhaps they can hold it for me there."

"And . . . as to the disposition of the remains? You are the next of kin."

"He might as well be buried there. I can see no point in shipping bodies around like freight. There was no place he really called home anyway."

"And . . . how shall I reply to the inquiry regarding his . . . ah . . . sexual proclivities?"

"Yes," Casey said. "It is possible he carried on homosexual affairs."

6 ***

WHEN CASEY FIRST MET CHARLES FORD he was part of the horde of returning veterans that swarmed onto the country's college campuses in the aftermath of World War II. Earnest young men, most of them, a few years older than most undergraduates, sustaining themselves on their dole from the G.I. Bill of Rights, sitting hunched over their books in overheated lecture halls in their Eisenhower jackets and army issue trousers. But there were many things about Charles Ford that set him apart from the others. First of all he was not a veteran. He was an immigrant with an Oxonian accent and a smooth Old World air about him. He was slightly shorter than medium height, slightly soft and chubby, carefully groomed, with hair that was beginning to thin at the age of twenty-two. His teeth were large and slightly protruding. His eyes were brown and bovine under a canopy of heavy, sleepy-looking lids. He wore no "Ike" jacket but the contemporary "bold look" style prescribed by *Esquire* magazine, and he flashed a diamond-studded signet ring on the little finger of his right hand. He rotated the ring back and forth on the axis of his finger constantly, catching the light with the little diamond.

The males on campus who knew him disliked him. Maybe it was his accent or his sharp clothes or the air of effete elegance he affected. Maybe it was because some of the best-looking girls in the school seemed so drawn to him, and the guys couldn't figure out why. He wasn't handsome. He wasn't an athlete. He wasn't even a scholar. But he exuded the air of a man with income potential. But to the girls of that time, who went to college to bring home a husband, the smell of a "winner" was attraction enough. Lacking any native gifts, he became the campus entrepreneur, organizing dances, pep rallies, beauty contests and varsity shows, capitalizing on the talents of others to achieve a special celebrity all his own.

He held court in a cafeteria down the street from the Square, sipping from a cup of coffee in one hand while the other roamed under the table, stroking the thigh of the lucky cheerleader who had maneuvered herself into the seat next to him. Thus enthroned he planned his pep rallies, homecoming dances, beauty contests . . . and "private" evenings at home. Those mysterious nights in his flat became the subject of titillating conjecture on the part of outsiders. Who went? What went on? Nobody who had been there had told. But among the uninvited there were cynics who boldly hinted that Ford paid his rent and financed his nocturnal activities by tapping the receipts of the campus functions he so assiduously promoted.

One day, in the second half of the semester, he astonished Casey by inviting her to join him, alone, for a cup of coffee. Since he had not so much as nodded to her during the entire course of the year, his invitation left her totally nonplussed. She knew she wasn't his type. She was neither flashy nor fawning but, rather, self-sufficient and awesomely intelligent. And she was half a head taller than he in her low-heeled saddle shoes. The truth was she didn't think she was *anyone's* type.

She was as emotionally naive as she was intellectually

*** **20**

precocious. He began to court her to the exclusion of all others, or so he led her to believe. He took her to the movies and taught her to dance. But though they became inseparable, he never invited her to his apartment. In those ingenuous days she mistook this for a sign of his esteem and respect for her.

He switched places in class with other students so that he could sit next to her. It wasn't until months later that she realized he was cribbing from her papers and copying from her homework books. When she remonstrated with him, he shrugged it off with the argument that none of this mattered anyway; he was merely biding his time, waiting for bigger things, things she would share with him one day. This petty cheating was the first and least of many disenchantments she was to experience in her relationship with him. It troubled her conscience, but she allowed it to go on. For she had fallen in love with him, though she really had no way of knowing what falling in love was all about. At the age of nineteen she had had absolutely no romantic experience against which she could gauge her feelings.

He infected her like a virus at a time when her resistance was low, and she had never really been able to throw him off. He curdled her emotional development and sensitized an area of feeling somewhere inside her so that twenty years later, no longer an impressionable girl, and knowing all she knew about him, she still responded to him. He was like a fever in her blood that kept recurring . . . until Mr. Walters called to inform her, gently, as a concerned family physician might, that the virus that was Charles Ford had been wiped out.

21 ***

7

THEY THREW A CHAMPAGNE PARTY for her at the office. It had become an annual event at five o'clock in the afternoon of the day before she took off on her European junkets, a kind of ritual anointing of the crusader sallying forth across the sea bearing the banner of McKormick-Bailey, publishers, into foreign lands. It was also an excuse for those left behind to get thoroughly sloshed. The big conference table on the twenty-sixth floor was covered with a festive cloth and laid end-to-end with trays of hors d'oeuvres, cardboard ice buckets, and bottles of champagne. A bright bower of crepe-paper streamers crisscrossed the ceiling. Everyone was there, from secretaries and office boys to owners and editors. At first they clustered in groups according to their station. Then the sporadic conversation and sudden empty silences slowly gave way to riotous cacophony as the champagne bottles emptied and the glasses filled and drained and filled again. The social barriers came down. The room became hazy with cigarette smoke and woozy with booze. A window was opened to let in air. The decibel level rose. Deodorants failed. And so did moral restraint, in the stairwells and closets adjoining the conference room.

Through it all Casey stood zombielike in a corner, isolated from the others in body and mind. Her face was a mask, her high-breasted sweatered torso sagged, her faded blue eyes were vacant. Zombielike she accepted the gushing good wishes of some of her colleagues and the thinly camouflaged bitchy conviviality of others. She made what passed for conversation where it was required of her. But she was really out of it, unaware even of how much she was drinking as the glass in her hand was repeatedly filled by passing hands. At one point Mr. Bailey, the chairman, surfaced long enough to ask her if she was feeling all right. She replied that she was fine, and he gratefully burrowed back into the noisy crowd. She was behaving according to form.

She had a reputation for being moody and capricious, sometimes so absorbed in her work that she remained uncommunicative for days, sometimes startling her co-workers with antic spells of mirthfulness.

When she had begun there nineteen years ago as an assistant reader her more lackadaisical and gregarious colleagues had nicknamed her "the bookworm." She had been a senior editor for over a decade now, but the label had stuck, applied with affection by those who were fond of her, with derision by those who weren't. She had her share of enemies: colleagues and competitors who were offended by her standoffishness or envious of her ability and her success. They were the ones who insinuated that perhaps her compassion for outsiders, her special interest in developing nascent talent, transcended the normal bounds of business. She was a woman, they winked, with womanly desires, and a woman of some power, though her physical attractiveness was fading. They were wrong, of course. She had no trouble satisfying her desires when she wanted to, or relieving her periodic and despairing spells of loneliness. But not with her authors. Any relationship of more than passing nature would have been too much for her to bear. This her detractors could never understand, not without understanding the bizarre and burdened adolescence that had shaped her, or the brief, disastrous marriage that had driven her into herself. Very few of the others even knew that she had once been married, since she was known about the place as *Miss* Ford. Certainly none of them knew of the visit she had had from Mr. Walters that morning.

She had come to work as usual, perhaps a little more remote than usual. She had dutifully attended the champagne party, though it was obvious that her mind was elsewhere. She would come back from Europe with contracts for foreign manuscripts that the others would wish they had found. But the company rarely sent the others overseas. They sent Casey Ford, "the bookworm."

SHE LEFT THE TALL OFFICE BUILDING and stood, coat open and blowing in the eddying winds of Rockefeller Plaza, a tall, slim-legged figure with a pouter pigeon torso. Too much sitting and too little exercise had given her of late a top-heavy look. She had tried a girdle and thrown it away, deciding instead to cut down on her calories by eating less and smoking more. But she smoked too much anyway when she was working and drank too much when she was alone, and that's where most of the excess calories came from. Still, at forty-two, she looked a lot sexier than she thought she did.

She stood there awhile, unmindful of the cold, head buzzing with wine and memories, absently watching the skaters tracing patterns on the ice in the rink down below. Then she turned and flagged a cab to take her home. Through some trick of the mind she gave the driver the address of the house in which she and Charles Ford had lived twenty years before. She sat in the cab, unseeing, as she was driven uptown, through neighborhoods that had metamorphosed with time. She paid the driver and stepped out in front of the building that had briefly been her home and stood, bewildered, on wobbly legs, wondering where she was and how she had come there. She'd have to watch her drinking habits, she thought, or she'd wind up like her old man. She held one hand out against the rough brick of the building for support. She found herself blinking back tears. Perhaps it was the wind. It came howling down the street from the park and took her breath away.

"You waiting for someone, lady?" A strapping young man in a soiled sheepskin jacket materialized at her side. He was hatless in the cold, and the wind blew through his thick hair, making it dance like anemones.

"I'm O.K. I just lived here once, that's all."

"You'll freeze out here. You want to come inside?" He looked at her strangely and it crossed her mind that he must know she was smashed.

"I'd better get home."

"Where's that?" he asked.

"I'll get a cab."

He took her arm and she didn't fight it. "Come on up. I'll make you a cup of coffee 'til you feel a little steadier on your feet."

"You live here?" she asked.

"Five-E."

"We had a view of the park," she said.

"Nobody has a park view here anymore. They built that high rise project on the other side."

"I see."

She allowed him to lead her to the lobby and into the elevator and up to Five-E, which faced on the courtyard. She sat on a straight-backed chair in the kitchen, shivering

25 ***

in her overcoat while he heated water for instant coffee. And then she let him take her overcoat off.

She stood and followed him as he took her hand and led her to the bed, all silent, all without a word between them. But she was thinking of the apartment on the other side of the building, the one with the park view where she had come to live with Charles. Poor Charles. And as she lay beneath the boy, her long legs limply spread, she thought how Charles would appreciate this. Wherever he was, she hoped that Charles was watching as she knew he had always liked to watch when he invited young men to perform the acts he was incapable of performing. She had learned the secret of Charles' apartment. As she passively let the boy slip a pillow under her (one of the few things in her life she had passively accepted), and as he slipped into her, she thought . . . "Dear Charles, wherever you are, it's just like old times, isn't it?"

8 ***

DORFF SAT IN THE DARK in his room in the Wild Boar Inn in Salisbury, watching the lighted window across the cobble-stoned courtyard. Its occupant was silhouetted behind the lacy curtains, occasionally rising and pacing, and then sitting down again; but never leaving the room, not even to go down to dinner.

Dorff squinted at the luminous dial on his wristwatch. It was getting late. It was going to be a long vigil. He decided he'd better call Rawlings in London and let him know what was going on. He picked up the phone and flashed the operator and waited while she got him the number.

"Rawlings here."

"Dorff."

"It's about time. What have you been up to?"

"Making inquiries. Discreetly, as you instructed. Discretion wastes a lot of time, you know."

"What about Ives?"

"He took off without leaving a trace. But the bastard set it up beautifully. He set the thing up just right to fit Ford's image."

"All right. Get a night's sleep and come back in tomorrow. We'll have to start from this end. I'll bring Wernicke and Handle in to help."

"I think I should stay awhile longer."

"To what end? Ives is certainly not going to show up in Salisbury again."

"No. But someone else has . . . Mrs. Ford."

There was a sudden silence, as if the line had gone dead.

"Are you still there?" Dorff asked.

"Yes." There was a strange, cold hollowness in Rawlings' voice when he came back on the line. "Did you say *Mrs.* Ford?"

"That's right." Dorff derived some satisfaction from the way his discovery had shaken the usually imperturbable Rawlings. "She showed up this afternoon, had a little chat with the police, accompanied what was left of Ford's body to the crematorium, and then visited with the police again."

"And what did her appearance do to their homosexual theory?"

"Apparently she confirmed it with whatever she told them. There was nothing in the late news to indicate the police had changed their minds. She's in a room across the courtyard from me now. Hasn't left it, not even for dinner. I want to get a look at what she's got in there."

"What makes you think she's got anything?"

"She left the police station with a small parcel. Personal effects, I would guess. But there might be something there to give us a lead."

"Apparently it gave the police no lead . . . or they wouldn't have let it go."

"They're not looking for what we're looking for. Do you want me to follow this up or don't you? You're in charge," Dorff said resentfully.

"I don't want uninvolved people hurt or we're liable to be dealing with more than just the local police. Be careful."

"I know my business," Dorff grumbled.

"Of course you do. But you tend to be physical in stress situations. She'll have to leave the room sometime. Be patient until then."

"If I were going to barge in on her, I'd have done it hours ago. I wouldn't be sitting here in the dark getting chilblains."

"Phone me as soon as you have something to report."

"That may require some patience on your part."

"Let's both be patient. Goodnight, Dorff."

"I'm sure it'll be a better night for you than for me," Dorff muttered resentfully and rang off.

9 ***

CASEY HAD ACCEPTED THE PARCEL containing Charles Ford's manuscript earlier that day, along with the urn containing his ashes. She had gone out with the ashes and scattered them on the plain. Then she had taken the manuscript, all that remained of Charles, back to her room at the Wild Boar Inn and had begun to read.

Ordinarily she was a rapid reader. She had to be. She could plow through an average length manuscript in a matter of two or three hours, judge its quality and potential, and either hold it for future study and development or dictate a letter of rejection.

But Ford's manuscript, though it was less than a hundred pages long, was so unsettling in so many ways that she found herself still reading, and rereading, well past midnight. The manuscript was scrawled entirely in longhand, and that had slowed her down, of course. But, more than that, it was so autobiographical in nature, though the name of the protagonist had been changed from Ford to Forster, and she recognized so much of herself as well as Charles in it that she found herself constantly stopping and remembering and matching up the fictional incidents with the real ones that had inspired them, and blinking back unaccustomed tears.

In the early pages of his manuscript Ford had synthesized their relationship into the story of a brother and sister roaming Europe in the aftermath of the Second World War, searching for remaining members of a vanished family . . . and a lost inheritance. They find pieces of the puzzle along the way: a fragment of a letter, scorched and incomplete, in the ruins of their old home; the name of a notary in Amsterdam who had served the family.

The odyssey of the fictional boy and girl through postwar Europe was almost identical in its itinerary to the stops she and Charles had made on their failed honeymoon twenty years before. On that journey, as in his story, he seemed to be questing after shadows.

As they traveled from the Mediterranean to the North Sea, her days had been filled with wonder and discovery. But her nights were troubled and restless. There were all the fabled sights she had dreamed about, and there was Charles by her side, courtly and attentive. But with nightfall he became preoccupied and withdrawn and often vanished for hours at a time, leaving her to toss, eaten by self-doubt, in her twin bed. He always insisted on twin beds wherever they stopped, despite the tightness of their budget and the fact that they were on their honeymoon. The truth was that their marriage had never been consummated. And he seemed to take it for granted that his disinterest along these lines was matched by her own.

She wondered if perhaps she should attempt to take the initiative in bed. She didn't dare. She wouldn't know quite how to begin. Having begun, she might face the crushing prospect of being rebuffed. Things were not bad as they were. Let it be. If he chose to think of her as a companion rather than as a lover, let it be. If his desire for her went no further than the need for someone to lean on, he fulfilled her need for someone to care for.

Then his absences became more frequent and more protracted. When she ventured to question him about them, he shrugged her off, claiming he had been trying to contact "friends" who might know if any of his family had survived the war. She wondered why he chose not to allow her to meet these "friends" but decided not to press the issue. Her insecurity was that great.

Once he vanished for two whole days, and when he came back they had their first bitter fight. He became very contrite and very affectionate, holding and petting her until she stopped crying and fell asleep. But their marriage remained unconsummated. And she wondered if this whole bewildering honeymoon trip had been undertaken as a vehicle from which he could pursue his search for a family that no longer existed. He had often joked that he hadn't married her for her money but for her passport. She began to wonder if it was true.

Ford's manuscript brought all this back. Most of it she was able to recall with detachment. It had all happened so long ago, and time had wrought such changes in her, that it might have happened to someone else.

But there was one scene in the story that not even the passage of time could shift into soft focus. It jolted her now as its real-life counterpart had jolted her twenty years ago. She was still a chronic victim of its after-shocks, particularly when her emotional equilibrium was upset. Its most recent manifestation had occurred two nights ago with the young man in the sheepskin jacket. In Ford's story, the sister, separated from her brother in the closing year of the war, falls into the hands of a marauding platoon of Soviet soldiers and is forced to submit to them, one by one, while an impotent officer cheers them on. The actual scene from which it had been synthesized took place in a cramped stateroom in tourist class on the ship that was bringing them home from their European honeymoon.

*** 32

They had made the acquaintance of a young man their age who was traveling alone: a tall, athletic young man with honey-colored hair and a delightfully carefree manner. He shared their table at dinner and their daily wager in the ship's lottery. They played bingo together in the tourist class lounge and had their deck chairs placed side by side. They danced to the music of the ship's orchestra, Charles and Eric taking turns with her on the dance floor. Eric paid her compliments which caused Charles to preen, and Eric's flattery delighted Casey. The thought that a man might consider her attractive was startling to her at that time.

They were a happy trio, she and Charles and their new-found friend Eric. And, strangely, Eric's presence seemed to have an aphrodisiac effect on both of them. She began to sense that Charles was feeling something for her beyond mere affection, beyond his respect for her intellect, beyond his need for her support. And coincidentally she was experiencing an awakening of desire she had never known before.

On their fourth night out, the night before they reached New York, she retired at about one o'clock in the morning feeling deliciously sleepy and tingling all over after an evening of games and dancing at the ship's gala ball. Charles and Eric had remained at the bar for a nightcap.

Perhaps she had only begun to doze in her bunk, or perhaps she had been asleep for a while, when she heard, far away, at the edge of consciousness, the click of the lock as their stateroom door opened.

"Charles?" she murmured and stretched and turned over on her side. She was vaguely conscious of fingers running under her hair at the back of her neck, and then there were lips where the fingers had been, warm and moist, and a thrill coursing through her.

33 *

"Charles," she murmured again, feeling languid and loose and vaguely wondering if she were dreaming. And then she knew she wasn't dreaming. It was happening. And suddenly the wanton looseness was gone and she became tense with the fear that perhaps she might fail him.

"Everything's going to be just beautiful," she heard Charles' voice whisper from somewhere far away. And the lips moving around to the side of her neck and the fingers reaching under the blanket and under her nightdress, stroking her belly, awakening strange and delightful sensations in her. And, as she became more and more awake, she wondered if it wouldn't be all the more delicious if she could remain half dreaming.

She felt a body, lean and hard, slip under the covers beside her and realized with alarm that Charles was neither that lean nor that long. She woke fully and turned and, in the residue of light that filtered in from around the door, defined Eric's features.

She gasped and recoiled until the iron bulkhead blocked her retreat from the bed. And there was Charles' voice again. "Don't be frightened, Casey. It's going to be just beautiful."

She saw Charles, a shadowy eminence, perched on the bed across from hers. Despite her panic and bewilderment the thought crossed her mind that Charles must be doing this out of his love for her. Still, she sat bolt upright, trapped against the bulkhead, pushing with her palms against Eric's steely chest.

She felt his hands come up inside her wrists and push them apart. His body and his lips were on her again. And his tongue was in her mouth as she opened it to protest. And his hand, always moving, erasing with each movement her strength, her will, her instinct to protest, filling her up

*** **34**

with another instinct . . . to melt, to open herself, to explode and release herself.

She slid back down on the bed and saw him leaning over her, and heard her hard breathing, and his . . . and Charles' on the opposite bed, all mixed up together. And felt him pressing for entry into the volcano he had stirred up inside her. A little cry escaped her as she flung her calves up and locked them across his back and hung there, impaled, her mouth against his . . . unheedful of Charles, unfeeling of shame, urging Eric on until the volcano erupted.

When the ship docked she and Charles went quietly to their apartment and said nothing of the events of the night before. And she thought that would be the end of it. But three nights later Charles invited Eric over, and, to her secret chagrin, she looked forward to the hour when the drinks and the small talk would be done. And she knew, even as she looked forward to it, that this would be the last time. She could live a celibate life with Charles, but there was something in her stronger than her awakened desires that forbade her to continue as a partner in his depravity. The next morning she told him she was leaving.

A year later Charles had begun sheepishly courting her again. They needed each other, he declared. But she had matured enough to realize that she need not spend the rest of her life caring for the morally crippled and emotionally maimed. She transferred her maternal instincts to the hopeful young authors besieging the publishing house where she had gone to work as an editorial trainee.

10 ***

DESPITE ALL ITS LITERARY FLAWS and the obvious haste in which it was written, Ford's story held her spellbound. She knew that this was partly because it opened a window on the enigma that had been her husband and partly because of the memories it evoked of incidents that had lain sleeping in her subconscious for years. But he also had an intriguing story to tell. The trouble was it was incomplete.

There were tantalizing sketches for a chapter about a gold-smuggling operation between Eastern Europe and the West. There were four or five vivid pages describing an arduous trek into the rugged backlands of an unnamed country in the tropics. There was a vague but promising scene in a government-controlled botanical lab where an agreement was made to perform a kind of alchemy in reverse . . . to convert gold into a more base and portable material. Casey wondered what this material could be. Charles' manuscript gave no clue. It told only two-thirds of a story. It had no ending.

There were chaotic notes scattered here and there among the pages: a chapter to be written about the hero's flight from shadowy pursuers . . . an attempt to meet a contact in Amsterdam . . . contact missed . . . pursuers too close . . . a flight to Switzerland and back to Amsterdam . . . a message waiting at Honeymoon Hotel. What a bizarre and improbable name for a Dutch hotel. Charles must have been thinking of Casey when he scribbled that note. They had spent two days of their honeymoon in Amsterdam at the rambling Hotel Krasnapolsky. The notes were that vague, that incoherent. They pointed no way to a resolution.

Casey went back to the manuscript and reread one of its most puzzling and provocative pages: *They might have been in a catacomb. But the recesses in the wall were filled with treasure instead of bones. Forster and the foreigner watched carefully as the attendant brought the boxes out of the wall, one by one. There were eight boxes in all. Four were full, four were empty. The four full, heavy boxes belonged to Forster. The empty ones belonged to the foreigner. The attendant stacked the boxes neatly and withdrew, leaving the two men alone.*

Forster opened the first of the four boxes belonging to him and gestured to the foreigner to look. The box was tightly packed with small golden ingots.

Together the two men emptied the full boxes and filled the empty ones. The gold now belonged to the foreigner and would reside in his recesses in the wall.

The foreigner then handed Forster a package. This was placed in one of the boxes belonging to Forster.

The attendant was summoned and returned the boxes to their respective places in the wall. The business at hand was complete. Forster's treasure would be safe for a while. But only if he could meet his contact in Amsterdam without alerting his pursuers!

Casey was perplexed. What had the gold been exchanged for? Who were the "pursuers"? The page was almost identical to and as ambiguous as the page he had sent her months before in the letter from Lugano when he had first declared his intention to write a novel. It must have served as the genesis for his story. Indeed, it had read like a beginning.

But here it was at the end, or as far as Charles had been able to go.

Ford's manuscript as it stood was no more than an aborted promise. But because it was Charles', because it was, in a sense, his only legacy, it presented Casey with a challenge and a dilemma. She had his crude chapters and sparse notes. She had some insight into the mind of the man who had written them. She could use her own imagination to fill in the empty spaces and achieve a resolution. After all, it was partly her story, too.

The poor bastard, she thought, with the ambivalence that had characterized her feeling for him for years. His manuscript was as promising as his life had been . . . and as incomplete.

She lit a cigarette and stared out the window at the ghostly silent dark streets of Salisbury in the early morning hours. She decided she would try to help him bring to fruition at least this one last thing.

IN THE DARKENED ROOM in the opposite wing of the Wild Boar Inn, Dorff sat in an armchair with his feet propped up on the bed. He reached over to the night table and dumped the contents of his overfull ashtray into a wastebasket. Then he opened a fresh pack of cigarettes and lit up. Judging from the movements of the silhouette in the window across the way, the woman was undressing for bed. He inhaled deeply and let his imagination flesh out the shadow as the woman stepped out of her skirt and pulled a sweater or blouse up over her head. He felt cheated as she stepped away from the window and the silhouette vanished. He was missing the best part. She would be taking off her brassiere now, rolling down her stockings. Then the lights went out.

*** **38**

He looked at the luminous dial on his wristwatch. It was almost four A.M. He doubted it was her grief that had kept her awake so long. She had certainly not seemed overly distraught when he had followed her from the crematorium. There must have been something in that parcel she had carried from the police station . . . something that had held her attention all these hours. Maybe it was just crammed with old photographs and letters. Maybe they had just put her in a nostalgic mood. But maybe there was something else. He would have to find out . . . in the morning. She had missed dinner. She would certainly have to go down to breakfast. He drew in deeply on the cigarette. It had grown so short it burned his lip. He cursed softly and ground it out.

11

THE SLEEPING STREETS of Salisbury came slowly awake with the buzz of Mini-Coopers, the clangor of trucks, the cries of a news hawker. Wednesday had turned Salisbury into a bustling market town.

Casey opened her eyes a little and was greeted by a bleak gray wintry light that barely penetrated the frosted-over window glass and lacy curtains. She snapped on the bedside lamp and squinted at her wristwatch lying face-up on the table. Eight o'clock. She'd slept barely more than four hours. She sat up in bed, and as her quilt and blankets fell away she found herself engulfed by a chill that set her teeth chattering. She pulled the quilt off the top of the bed and wrapped it around her as she searched for her purse for a coin and matches. Wearing her quilt like a toga, she tip-toed gingerly across the frigid floor, put the coin into the slot, and lit the gas heater. Then she hurried back to bed. She lay there awhile under the covers, giving the heater a chance to take the chill out of the room. Then she dressed in her warm woolen slacks of oatmeal tweed, a heavy turtle-neck sweater and oxford walking shoes, and went down to breakfast.

A gleaming Rolls Royce and a couple of staid Humber sedans were parked out in the cobblestoned courtyard where horses had clattered in centuries gone by, in the days when the inn was a coach stop on the main road from the North.

A tall, macabre ebony clock, carved with skulls and hooded scythe-bearing figures by some Victorian medievalist, gloomily chimed the quarter hour as she came into the foyer.

Businessmen decked out like diplomats in a 1930s newsreel milled about in morning coats, striped trousers, wing collars and club ties, waiting for a table or for their tablemates. She wondered if, in the bizarre setting, she might not be more of an anachronism in her simple sweater and slacks than the businessmen in their tails and striped trousers.

Off to the side of the lobby, in a smoking room furnished with green velour lounge chairs and small side tables, a big, brawny, rumpled man in a raglan coat sat sipping coffee and wolfing down cold toast and marmalade. His tweed fedora rested on the table along with the coffee pot and the silver toast caddie. She wondered if she ought to take her breakfast in the smoking room where, it appeared, the tweedy people sat. But the hostess, scanning the milling crowd in the lobby, held up a finger indicating a single available in the dining room and then waggled it at Casey. As Casey started for the dining room, she caught a glimpse of the man in the raglan coat as he laid a piece of half-finished toast on top of his coffee cup, picked up his hat and fished in his pocket for coins to pay the bill.

CASEY came out of the dining room thirty minutes later, after stoking up on a breakfast of blood pudding and sausage. A new group of hungry businessmen had gathered in the lobby. The Rolls and the Humbers had left the courtyard and had been replaced by Austins and Rovers. The man in the raglan coat was still sitting in the anteroom, his tweed hat on the table. Yet Casey was sure she had seen

41 ***

him preparing to leave earlier. The coffee pot and tea caddie had been removed and an ashtray set in their place. The man stubbed out his cigarette and rose, leaving his hat on the table. He caught up with Casey as she started up the stairs to her room.

"Mrs. Ford?" She was still unaccustomed to being addressed as "Mrs." after all these years, although the police and the funeral director had done so yesterday. She turned.

"I'm Inspector Corning, Salisbury police. I was out yesterday when you came in. First, let me say how sorry I am about Mr. Ford. I take it you were his only family."

"In a way, yes. But we've been separated for a long time."

He was taken aback by her undecorous reluctance to make a show of mourning.

"I understand, of course. But you have maintained contact with him over the years, haven't you?"

"We remained on friendly terms."

"I thought so. One wouldn't leave a parcel, as he did, to someone from whom he was totally estranged."

"What is this all about, Inspector?"

"I just wondered if I might take a few more moments of your time. Loose ends, you know . . . loose ends to be tied up neatly. We could talk in your room . . . or in the anteroom if you'd prefer."

"I could use a cigarette, if you have one, Inspector." Corning nodded, and she followed him into the smoking lounge.

"Would you care for a cup of tea?" he asked as he drew up a chair for her close to the table on which his hat rested.

"I've just had breakfast, thanks. But I could use some coffee, if you don't mind. Black, please."

Corning rang for the waiter.

When the order had been given—black coffee for the

lady, tea with milk for himself—Corning placed his elbows on the table and leaned across his hat, bringing his face close to Casey's in a confidential manner. His face might have once been handsome, despite the pockmarks along the jaw line. They might not have been so noticeable at one time, before the weight of middle age and waxing jowl had stretched them into angry pink craters. It was still a strong face, one of those rough-hewn masculine faces that seem not to suffer from their owner's having gone bald. In fact, it was difficult to imagine what he might have looked like with a full head of hair; perhaps less commanding, less strong. The eyes were small for a face that size, and they squinted as if they were nearsighted or bothered by too much smoke. They were red-rimmed and irritated, and there were pouches beneath the lower lids. They were the eyes of a man suffering from a heavy head cold or a lack of sleep.

He studied her with his tired red eyes, trying to decide on the best way to begin the business at hand. Casey decided to help him.

"You said you had a cigarette, Inspector."

Corning blinked, as if brought back from some reverie. "Of course. How thoughtless of me." He had extremely long and lovely eyelashes, Casey thought. They didn't fit the face or eyes. He reached into his side pocket and brought out a black and gold cardboard cigarette box. "I'm afraid you might find these rather strong. I can have the waiter bring you others if you like."

Casey recognized the box. "Sobranie!"

"You've had them before?"

"I've been around a bit. Balkan tobacco, right?"

"Yes," Corning said, and then apologetically, "something of an extravagance. But then a man should allow himself a few luxuries. I find our Virginia tobaccos, and yours too, somewhat like smoking straw." He rolled his *r*'s heavily, and Casey tried to place the accent. Scotland? Wales? It certainly wasn't B.B.C. English.

Casey took a cigarette from the proffered box, and Corning lit it with a hand the size of a boulder. Then he tucked his cigarettes and matches away and leaned across his hat again.

"Now I suppose I should explain why I've taken the liberty of intruding on your privacy this morning."

"I had nothing else to do, Inspector. I'm just waiting for the noon train."

"You're leaving so soon?" he asked. Casey wondered why almost every question a policeman asked, no matter how innocent, seemed to bear overtones of suspicion or accusation.

"I have nothing to keep me here, Inspector. And I have business in London and on the Continent."

"I'm glad to see you're carrying on so well." Again the note of accusation. Or was it all in her mind?

"I told you before, Inspector. Charles and I had not lived together for a long, long time."

The waiter brought the coffee and the tea and set them on the table beside Corning's tweed hat.

"But you did see each other occasionally?"

"Yes."

"And your meetings were amicable? You harbored no bitterness against Mr. Ford?" Again the accusatory tone.

"Of course not. Not after all these years." Casey sipped her coffee.

"Then you were embittered once?"

"I was crushed. I was too naive to be bitter then."

Casey stubbed out her half-smoked cigarette. Corning looked for a moment as if he'd like to rescue the remains.

*** **44**

"He was really a most unhappy and unfortunate person. Anyway, I've never felt bitter toward him. Annoyed with him, yes. Disappointed with him, sorry for him. Yes! But never bitter."

"Might I ask what the cause of your initial difficulty was?"

"You might. But I won't answer. It was long ago."

"It might shed some light on the manner of his passing."

"I told them yesterday all about that. I don't care to go into it again."

"I'm sorry. As you know, I wasn't there yesterday. I was out doing some . . . field work . . . some research into some of his . . . ah . . . questionable activities. I hope you won't mind my being so frank."

"It seems to me you're being evasive. Are you leading up to the sexual thing again?"

"I'm referring to the financial thing."

Casey shook her head and smiled, sympathetically. "Which one?"

"Ah! Then you were aware of these?"

"Of course. I had to help bail him out of enough of them."

"Were you aware of *all* his involvements?" There was that accusing tone again, as if she were an accomplice.

Casey gulped down the last of her coffee. "I doubt it." And then, defensively. "Look. I resent your implying that I should have gone into all this with the officer who talked to me yesterday. The man's gone, that's all there is to it. It's quite plain what happened to him. Maybe it was bound to happen that way. If he still owes someone money, they'll just have to write it off as a bad debt. I was moved to help him when he was alive. But I won't go into hock to protect his memory."

Corning leaned across the table very close to her and

45 ***

said, very softly but very intensely, "This is not a matter of a bad gambling debt, Mrs. Ford, or even of a minor defalcation. We know all about those. It occurred to us, or rather to me, quite late I must admit, that perhaps he might have attempted to repay you in some way for the favors you had done him."

"Repay me with what?" Casey asked testily. She was becoming annoyed with this interrogation and with its implications. She was anxious to bring the interview to a close. "Charles had very grandiose ideas, but he lived barely hand to mouth most of his life. He had a sure-fire scheme for every week of the year, and as far as I know nothing ever came of any of them."

"I think you are more upset by all this than you may realize," Corning said unctuously.

The son of a bitch was reading her mind. "I would just like to get this over with and get back to my room. I spent a rather sleepless night, and I have traveling to do today."

"Would it surprise you, Mrs. Ford, if I told you there was a very large amount of money involved here?"

"It would surprise me very much. And I still would be unable to see what it has to do with Charles' death."

"It is an amount of sufficient size to motivate murder, an amount in excess of a hundred thousand pounds." Casey's jaw dropped. She stared at Corning in disbelief. "That would be something around a quarter of a million dollars in your money."

"I know the rate of exchange," Casey snapped. "But I think you're way off the track. Wealth, or the pursuit of it, was an obsession with Charles. He felt he had no personal identity without it. He wanted it so badly that he pretended he had it even when he didn't. It was the only yardstick by which he could measure his manhood. It so obsessed him that his only creative effort outside his business machina-

*** 46

tions was a self-constructed fantasy in which there is a fortune in gold waiting for him somewhere . . . if only he could find it. I assure you, Inspector Corning, that if Charles had ever actually had his hands on a quarter of a million dollars he would have kept it no secret. He would have advertised it. He would have lived like a pasha. He would have seen to it that the whole world knew about it."

"Funny you should mention gold, Mrs. Ford."

"I mentioned it merely symbolically."

"Still . . . it's gold that's missing."

"Whose gold, Inspector?" Casey asked dubiously.

"That remains to be determined. Certainly not Mr. Ford's by any right of legal ownership."

"I think you're letting your imagination run away with you, Inspector."

"Perhaps. But you might bring me back to reality if you could tell me something about that parcel he left you. You've examined it, of course."

"Of course."

"And you found no bank account there, no solicitor's name, nothing at all that might indicate my theory is correct?"

"Don't you think your colleagues went through that parcel before they gave it to me?"

"Of course . . . but they didn't know him as well as you do. You might have noted something that would have escaped them completely."

"The package he left behind contained the manuscript for a novel, a piece of fiction, Inspector, nothing more. And even that, like everything else he attempted, was not quite complete."

"This . . . piece of fiction . . . I assume is the creative effort you mentioned a few moments ago."

"That's it. Now if you will excuse me."

47 ***

"Certainly, Mrs. Ford." Corning stood up politely. "I'm sorry to have troubled you in this way. Just a shot in the dark, you understand."

"I understand. Thanks for the coffee and the smoke." She started for the door.

"Mrs. Ford . . ." He stopped her. "Would you be so kind as to give me your address in London?" So she still wasn't off the hook. ". . . just in case we should like to reach you, you understand."

"I understand. I'll be at the Charing Cross."

"Thank you, Mrs. Ford."

"Good morning, Inspector."

She left him standing in the entrance to the anteroom. The lobby had emptied of breakfasting businessmen. In the courtyard only a Rover sedan remained. She went up to her room. She was tired and more shaken up than she had thought.

The chambermaids had been in the room. Everything was tidy and the bed had been made up. She began to pack her bags and found that her hands were trembling. She went to the dresser where she had left her flask the night before. She poured a couple of fingers of bourbon into the drinking glass on the washbasin. She downed the liquor in two shuddering gulps. It didn't help. Her blood was still racing. She felt uneasy and disoriented. Partly it was jet lag. She had landed in London just a little over twenty-four hours ago after an overnight flight from New York. In the interim hours she had seen to the disposal of Charles' remains and read his manuscript, and had very little sleep again. And this morning there had been the unpleasant question and answer session with Inspector Corning.

Her head began to throb. She opened her small overnight bag and searched for her bottle of aspirin. She filled the

*** **48**

drinking glass with tap water, shook two aspirin tablets out into her palm, cupped them to her mouth and swallowed them down. She finished packing her bags, keeping out only the small travel alarm clock, which she set for noon. That would give her ample time to get down to the station and catch the one o'clock train for London. Then, in the clothes she had breakfasted in and would travel in, she lay down on the freshly made bed and closed her eyes.

12 ***

SHE DOZED FITFULLY in the prenoon hours, half wakened at times by the sounds from the street and by the thumping and bumping noises from above as the chambermaids went about their work on the next floor. The room was cold too —too cold for comfort—and she had no more coins in her purse for the heater. She knew that if she went down to the desk in search of change she'd never get back to sleep again. Somnambulistically she reached down to where her overcoat lay folded atop one of the suitcases. She pulled it up over her shoulders and over her head. The coat kept out the cold and the workaday noises of the street and hostelry. Thus cocooned, she drifted off again.

She dreamed of two bodies lying naked side by side on sterile pallets. One was Charles and the other was she. She was both observer and participant in this bizarre vision. She reached across to touch Charles—he seemed so alone—and her hand recoiled as she touched a figure as cold and smooth and unyielding as one of the polished marble effigies on the tombs in Salisbury Cathedral. She touched herself, her face, her thighs, her breasts, and was horrified to discover that, though her flesh had not yet turned to stone, she was as cold and as bereft of life as Charles. Shuddering, she found herself awake. She sat bolt upright in the bed, jolted by the dream, trembling with the chill in the room, hugging herself for warmth. She got out of the bed and put her arms through the sleeves of her coat and buttoned it up. She got her cigarettes out of her purse and lit one, as if the inhaled smoke would warm her. She recalled the chronic nightmares that had tormented her as an adolescent for months after her father's death. She wondered how long Charles would haunt her that way. She sat down in a chair by the window and stared out at the cobblestoned courtyard, empty of cars now and slick with drizzle. Her thoughts kept returning to Charles and his manuscript, try as she might to shut them out. Corning's interrogation had disturbed her . . . upset her and opened up something in her.

Resigned, she got out of the chair and crossed the room to where her packed suitcases lay. She snapped open the suitcase into which she'd packed Charles' manuscript, brought it out, opened the manila envelope, and began scanning the pages, searching out the paragraphs that had stuck in her mind from the night before. Buried in the fiction and fantasy of Charles Ford's story were nuggets of detail that read like entries in a diary. A tortuous smuggling operation. Gold transported across borders, pound by pound, trip by trip, in little ingots. The steamy forests of a nameless tropical country. Negotiations. A trade agreement arrived at. The cumbersome gold exchanged for something easily portable. A package of what for all that gold? Flight across continents from shadowy pursuers. An attempt to meet a contact in Amsterdam. A note left at the Hotel Krasnapolsky.

Corning had said, ". . . there are things only you would know about him." Certainly she knew enough about him to wonder if he had written a memoir rather than a novel. She knew the early parts of his story were autobiographical. It occurred to her now that perhaps the latter parts were also true. If they were, then he had found the rainbow's end that had eluded him most of his life. And she was glad

51 ***

that he had had that satisfaction, at least, before he had died. But then, according to his manuscript, he had been hounded and pursued. And murdered? Yes! The thought stunned her. Murder would have been the inevitable end of his unfinished story. But not in a lovers' quarrel, as the police surmised.

He must have known that he might not survive, and had prepared this manuscript for her, coded so that only one who knew him as she knew him could perceive its meaning: a cryptic Baedeker meant to lead her to his coveted treasure as surely as Homer's *Iliad* had led Schliemann to the buried walls of Troy.

She sat on the bed in a daze, turning the pages of the manuscript without really seeing them, wondering if she was onto something or just fantasizing; groping for a meaningfulness in Charles' manuscript that had never been evident in his life.

The travel alarm went off, jarring her out of her reverie. And only then did it occur to her that whatever Charles had found and left behind, if indeed he had found anything, might not have been his to find or leave. She recalled Inspector Corning's visit with her in the anteroom . . . and his insinuations . . . and a wave of bitterness came over her.

Charles was saddling her with the consequences of his indiscretions even from the grave. If she wasn't fantasizing, if there was something in the manuscript, Corning and his colleagues had a right to know.

She looked at the clock. If the police chose to question her again she would miss her train . . . and her first appointment in London. No matter. It was her responsibility to call Corning and let him decide if there was anything to her suspicions. She picked up the phone and signaled the desk and asked them to ring up the police station.

*** 52

"Is there some trouble, ma'am?" the hotel operator asked in alarm.

"Not at all," Casey assured her. "Just some personal business to clear up." She hoped the operator wouldn't eavesdrop to be sure there was nothing that might embarrass the Inn. She waited while the connection was being made, a thought crossing her mind. Why should I tell them? If there is something hidden, he wanted me to have it. And then she dismissed the thought because, I'm not Charles. And then, almost wistfully, while she heard the phone ringing at the other end, but how exciting it would have been to have found Charles' Troy.

She heard the click as the phone was picked up at the other end.

"Police. Sgt. Daley here."

In a panicky flash it occurred to her that she might just be making a fool of herself. She was tired and emotionally distraught.

"Sgt. Daley here," the crisp male voice repeated.

She *was* fantasizing. She had better hang up, catch her train, and forget the whole thing.

"May we help you?" Sgt. Daley inquired commandingly.

"May I speak to Inspector Corning?" she heard herself saying.

There was a pause at the other end of the line. What is the matter with me? she wondered. Why should I read such a thing into Charles' manuscript? They must have gone through it before they gave it to me and they found nothing. They found nothing out of the ordinary despite Inspector Corning's insinuations that Charles had been dealing in contraband gold. Still, they didn't know Charles as she did.

"To whom did you say you wished to speak?" Sgt. Daley asked, puzzlement in his voice.

"Inspector Corning." Her voice caught in her throat.

"That's what I thought you said, ma'am. I'm afraid there is no Inspector Corning here. May I help you?"

"Do you know when he'll be in?" Casey asked.

"We have no one by that name on this staff," Sgt. Daley replied. "Would you care to speak to another officer?"

A chill ran through her beyond any cold she felt in the room. She thrust the receiver back into its cradle, breaking the connection. Her heart was pounding. She needed time to think, to evaluate. She wanted to flee. She took a deep breath, counted to ten, and again signaled the operator.

"This is Miss Ford in room 32. Please send a porter up for my bags and ask the desk to have my bill ready. I'll be leaving immediately."

"Certainly, ma'am." If the operator had been listening in on her call to the police she gave no sign.

*** 54

13 ***

IF INSPECTOR CORNING wasn't Inspector Corning, then who in hell was he, Casey wondered as she sat nervously over a half-empty teacup in the snack shop on the platform in Salisbury station. Her tongue had been scorched senseless by the scalding tea; her throat was burned raw from the hot Virginia cigarettes she'd been smoking in a chain since she'd arrived in the station twenty minutes too early for the train.

Of course, it might all be quite innocent. He might have been a bond salesman sniffing out a widow's wealth with the prospect of a large commission in mind. He might have been a journalist masquerading as a policeman to pry loose a story. He might have been a police inspector, after all. Perhaps she had misunderstood his name when he introduced himself.

Casey kept glancing up and down the platform, as if she expected to see Corning lurking in the shadow of a pillar or crouched behind a baggage cart. She knew she wouldn't. Her better judgment told her so. Her better judgment also warned her that she had not seen the last of him. She wished she hadn't given him the name of her hotel in London. She would have to find a room elsewhere. And the unsettling question remained. If there was no Inspector Corning, then who was the man who had interrogated her at the Wild Boar Inn?

DORFF WAS IN THE PHONE BOOTH on the platform across from where Casey sat waiting for the train. Dorff, too, was impatient and on edge. He had been in the phone booth for almost ten minutes, ever since he had followed Casey into the station. He'd rung the number three times already and there had been no answer at the other end. A hell of a time, he thought, for Rawlings to be out taking the air. Typical of Rawlings, he thought. Everybody else was expected to be available at the snap of a finger. But where the hell was he?

Dorff had seen Casey enter the snack shop across the tracks. He had guessed that she was waiting for the one o'clock train to London. He glanced at his watch. He'd wait five minutes more and then, with or without Rawlings' instructions, he'd have to move. He tried the London number again. It rang just once before Rawlings picked up at the other end. Dorff deposited his coins to complete the connection.

"Where are you?" Rawlings snapped.

"On the platform in Salisbury station, wondering when you'd decide to answer your phone."

"I waited through most of the morning to hear from you. Then I could wait no longer. I went to the loo."

"You have my sympathy. I sat up 'til nearly four this morning watching her window across the courtyard. She was up that late with something. But she never left the room. She went down to breakfast this morning, though. I got a quick look then, but not nearly as thorough as I like to be. I wasn't in there five minutes before I heard the chambermaids start working on the floor. Had to step out fast."

"Did you find anything?"

"I'm not sure. You're the specialist on Ford, maybe you know. Was he a writer?"

*** 56

"A rider?" Rawlings asked, puzzled. "You mean a horseman?"

"A writer. Of books. An author."

"He was a bloody chameleon. But as far as I know the only thing he ever wrote was a false stock prospectus. Why?"

"There were a half dozen of what looked like manuscripts in her luggage and some correspondence with publishers . . ."

"That would be Mrs. Ford's stuff. She works for a publishing house."

"I managed to figure that out by myself, thank you. But one of those manuscripts in the luggage was written by Ford. *Rainbow's End,* he called it. And there's a gushy little dedication on the first page. 'To Casey in the hope she will remember.' "

"That doesn't sound like Ford."

"It had his name under the title."

"Why would a man on the run take the time to write a book?"

"That's what I wondered, too. And it looked like he wrote it on the run, all right. All scrawled in pencil. Didn't even take the trouble to type it up like the other manuscripts."

"Did you read any of it?"

"I told you I only had a few minutes in the room. I looked at a bit of the first page. More mush. About a couple of orphan kids, it seemed."

"Did you find anything else?"

"Nothing except the usual female equipment . . . plus a pint flask. Bourbon from the smell of it."

"That doesn't sound right. She's not a drinker."

"Well, maybe you'd better update your dossier on her. There wasn't enough to bathe in. And there was too much gone for her to be daubing it behind her ears."

57 ***

"Do you suppose all that was in that parcel the police gave her was this manuscript of his?"

"It might have been. Or she might have had it before. If Ford left her anything else in that parcel she must be carrying it on her person."

"I wonder," Rawlings said.

"I only had a few minutes in the room. But it wasn't as if I had to search an entire flat." Dorff was on the defensive again. "I saw everything that was there . . . unless she slipped it into the lining of her luggage."

"Where is she now?" Rawlings asked.

"On the platform across from me. I think she's waiting for the London train."

"I'd like to get a good look at that manuscript of Ford's."

"I could grab her bag. I know which one it's in."

"Don't. Follow her and find out where she's stopping in London."

"What about Ives?"

"That manuscript may be our shortcut to Ives and the gold. Follow her and then report to me. Don't do anything overt. Understood?"

Three shrill whistles penetrated the phone booth. "That's the London train coming in," Dorff said.

He could see the train just entering the far end of the yards. He saw Casey Ford leave the snack bar, carrying her own bags. She set them down on the platform, one on each side of her and waited with the sprinkling of other passengers for the train to come in. There would be still a couple of minutes wait . . . enough time for Dorff to sprint down the stairs, through the underground, and onto the opposite platform just before the train left.

"Are you still there?" Dorff asked.

"I'm here. But you'd better get cracking."

*** 58

"There's time," Dorff said coolly. "But there's one more thing you should know. After I finished in her room, I went down to the smoking room for a cup of tea and some toast ... and I saw her there."

"Did she see you?" Rawlings asked, alarmed.

"No. She had her eyes down and I did a quick about-face. But I was there long enough to notice that she was having a little tête-à-tête with a big, burly bloke."

"A copper?"

"Might have been. He was facing the other way. But I don't think he was one of the ones who was with her yesterday. He was too big."

"If he wasn't a copper, who was he, then?"

"I'd feel a lot easier if I knew," Dorff said as he watched Casey get into a compartment in the fourth car back from the engine. He hung up the phone and began his dash for the underground and the opposite platform.

14 ***

CASEY SAT IN HER COMPARTMENT staring out at the bleak wintry countryside. The distance from Salisbury to London wasn't great—a matter of seventy or eighty miles. But the trip took hours, the train stopping interminably at dozens of small stations along the way: Andover . . . Basingstoke . . . Farnborough. . . . In late spring or summer the trip was a delight, she knew, through fields verdant and manicured as golfing fairways, past small houses with gardens in blossom, blossoms as big as grapefruits and so bright in the humid greenhouse climate of high summer that the first time she saw them she had wondered if they were real. The open station platforms, so dismal in winter, would be gaily festooned with potted plants, and there would be the lazy hum of bees.

But now the land and the station platforms were dead and cold and dark. She had planned to spend her hours on the train reading through Ford's manuscript again. But, though she had opened her suitcase and taken it out, she couldn't read. Her mind had become too clotted with memories.

Their marriage had been so brief . . . and its impact on her had been so lasting. He had never really let her go, nor had she ever entirely exorcised him. There had been the periodic, almost chronic letter from him . . . pleading for a short-term loan to bail him out of some temporary difficulty;

a gambling loss, an overdrawn check . . . once, even, money for clothes for a series of meetings he deemed important. Always, the affluence and position that he had pursued so fervently through so much of his life seemed just beyond reach.

The manuscript had reawakened memories of all of that and of her several encounters with him over the years after their marriage had ended. At times he had been ebullient and charming. At other times he had been morose and despondent. Two years ago, in Rome, he had been pathetic. A fictional synthesis of that incident was in the book too, very well camouflaged, but recognizable to her. How could she ever forget it?

She had been in Rome on business, as usual. She had sat down at a table at Doney's on the Via Veneto for a drink before returning to her room. She was startled to see Ford sitting a few tables away, his profile to her, facing an epicene elderly man whose shopworn elegance gave him the look of a down-at-the-heels aristocrat. She had not even known that Ford was in Italy.

The elderly man had his hand on Ford's, palm down on the table, and leaned coquettishly close to Ford as he spoke to him. Then the hand moved under the table, squeezing Ford's thigh, as Ford had done to the pretty cheerleaders in college so many years before. Casey had finished her drink quickly and asked for the check, hoping that she could leave before Ford saw her and suffered embarrassment. But as she paid her bill and stood up to go, Ford's tablemate laughed and patted Ford's cheek and pointed to someone passing in the street.

Ford turned to look and his eyes met Casey's, widening in astonishment and chagrin. Casey stood there, nonplussed, as Ford held up his hand signaling for her to wait.

61 ***

He excused himself from his companion and stumbled against a chair as he wove his way unsteadily through the maze of tables to her side.

"Why didn't you let me know you were in Rome?" he asked, thick-tongued and reproachfully, to compensate for his embarrassment.

"Just a few days on business. I didn't know you were here."

"You'll have to forgive me—I'm slightly smashed. Have to be to put up with that old fag. You took in the scene, I suppose."

"No need to apologize, Charles," Casey said.

"Just don't want you to get the wrong idea."

"I wasn't thinking a thing."

"He's a very important contact, you understand. It could mean a great deal to me."

"I understand."

"How long'd you say you'd be in Rome?"

"Just a couple of days."

"We'll have to get together soon's I wrap this one up. Where you staying?"

She gave him the name of her hotel down the street.

"Let me introduce you before you go. He's a count. An amateur botanist. Very highly respected in his field. Very well connected all over the world."

"It's not necessary, Charles."

"I think it's better if I do. He'll be impressed, you being in publishing. He writes poetry, too, he tells me."

She followed Charles back to the table, and he introduced her to the count, not bothering to mention that she was his former wife, but emphasizing that she was a very important editor at a big American publishing house. The count, watery-eyed, slack-lipped, and redolent of cologne, stood and leaned like a wilting reed across the table, taking

*** 62

her firm hand in his limp one and smacking his lips in the air an inch above her knuckles in a simulated kiss.

"I'll phone you," Charles muttered to her as he guided her back to the exit. But he didn't call, at least not during her two remaining days in Rome. That was typical of him.

That time in Rome was the last time she had seen him alive.

Casey could not bring herself to look at the manuscript again, not this day anyhow. The manuscript and the memories it evoked, and the visit from "Inspector" Corning and the disquiet it provoked, had left her exhausted. She had first imagined that Charles had left the manuscript to her as an offering of love. But she should have known, as she read it, as she certainly knew now, that Charles did nothing in a pure or simple or straightforward way. He was leaning on her posthumously now as he had done through all the years she had known him . . . and she resented it bitterly. But she didn't want to think about that now. She had business engagements in London tomorrow. She didn't want to think about them either. She wanted to get to a hotel in London, any hotel but the one whose name she had given to Corning, soak in a warm bath, then sleep through the long winter night.

"Woking" . . . "Wimbledon" . . . "Battersea Park" . . . "Victoria." She stepped down out of the train into the echoing cavern of the station. She waited on the platform with her bags for a porter. Ordinarily if there were no porters immediately at hand she would have carried the bags herself. But this afternoon she felt she didn't have the strength. She waited.

"SHE TOOK A TAXI from the station to the Cardigan up near Piccadilly. It looked to me like she had no reservation.

There was some confusion and searching about by the people at the reception desk until they settled on a room for her. I followed her up. Sixth floor. Number six-seventy-eight." Dorff finished his report, put his drink down on the marble-topped side table, got up out of his chair and stretched. He was still in his overcoat. He said, "I'd like to get a little rest now if you don't mind."

"Of course," Rawlings said absently. "Get a good night's sleep. I won't be needing you until tomorrow."

"You said before you thought we should have a look at that manuscript."

"I'll want to think about that some more. I'll call you in the morning."

"What if she decides to check out during the night? Someone should watch the hotel."

"Someone will," Rawlings said in that patronizing schoolmaster's tone that Dorff had grown to resent. "I've brought in Wernicke and Handle."

Dorff grunted. He was thinking that someday soon there was going to be a reckoning. He left the room without another word.

15 ***

IT WAS NINE-THIRTY THE FOLLOWING MORNING when Rawlings' Bentley drew up across from the Cardigan and glided into a parking space against the curb. Rawlings and Dorff sat in the back. Wernicke, dressed in chauffeur's livery, was driving. Wernicke turned off the ignition and pointed to a small Austin parked at the opposite corner. "There's Handle's car. Over there."

"Where the bloody hell is Handle?" Dorff grumbled sanctimoniously. The bugger had probably gone off for a hot drink and left the place unwatched.

"He's in the lobby," Rawlings answered coolly. "He called in about an hour ago when the place began waking up. He went in and waited for her to come down to breakfast. She's in the dining room now."

Dorff snorted. "The traffic wardens have done a proper job on him since he left the car. His windscreen's plastered over with summonses."

The telephone in the car buzzed abruptly. Rawlings picked it up. "Handle?"

"Where are you now?" Handle asked.

"Just across from the hotel."

"Good. She may be coming out any minute now. She just finished breakfast and returned to her room."

"You can go home, Handle," Rawlings said, "and thanks. We'll take over from here." Dorff noted resentfully that Rawlings was far more civil with the other men than with him.

"Thank you. I still haven't thawed out from sitting up all night in that damned car."

"You may find a traffic summons or two on your windscreen. Don't neglect to pay the fines. You can send me the bill."

"Ta. But that won't be necessary. I put them there myself. They keep the traffic wardens away." Handle rang off.

Rawlings hung up the phone and turned to Dorff. "He put the traffic summonses there himself. They keep the wardens away." Dorff looked stricken. "We'll wait until she leaves," Rawlings continued. "Then you let yourself into her room and bring Ford's parcel down to me. Do it neatly, now. We don't want to leave any signs of a break-in."

"Don't you worry about my technique. Just hope they don't have more than one lock on that door."

"They won't," Rawlings assured him. "This is London, not New York."

Handle came out of the hotel, sleek and foppish in a wasp-waisted coat and bell-bottomed trousers. His eyes took in Rawlings' Bentley as he hurried across the street, but he made no sign of recognition. He slipped the parking tickets out from under his windshield wiper, slipped them carefully into his inside breast pocket, got into the Austin, and drove off.

Wernicke took a paperback book out of his pocket, turned to a page with a corner folded down, and began to read. Rawlings smoked and watched the passers-by panting up from the deep stairways of the underground, hurrying to their jobs, briefcases in hand, shoulders hunched against the cold, breath condensing into mist. Dorff kept his eyes riveted on the hotel. He was the only one of the three who could identify Casey Ford.

*** 66

It was nine-fifty by the clock on the dashboard of the Bentley when Casey loped out of the hotel, carrying her purse over her shoulder and an attaché case in one hand, and clutching her coat collar up around her neck for warmth. A doorman followed in her wake, whistling for a cab. A cab drew up. The doorman held the door. Casey tossed her attaché case into the back seat and climbed in after it, neatly slipping a coin into the doorman's hand as she did so. The set of Rawlings' mouth softened with the trace of a smile.

Rawlings waited until the cab was well away and the doorman had returned to his station just inside the hotel lobby. Then he nodded to Dorff. Dorff got out of the car without a word and strode briskly across the street and into the hotel. Five minutes later he was on his way back, carrying a large manila envelope under his arm. He handed the manila envelope through the window to Rawlings, opened the door and got into the car. "You were right," he said. "They only had one lock on the door."

"Where to now?" Wernicke asked.

"We'll stay right here while I look through this thing." Rawlings opened the envelope and drew out an inch-thick packet of unbound papers. He riffled the pages with his thumb. "Busy little bee, our Mr. Ford, wasn't he?" Rawlings turned to Dorff. "You didn't note, by any chance, if she'd left an appointment calendar lying about?"

"I didn't see any," Dorff replied. "Why?"

"It might have given us an idea when she'll be back. But never mind. You keep your eye on that hotel entrance. The moment you see her returning, sing out, and be prepared to get this package back into her room as quickly as you brought it out."

"She'll be one step ahead of me," Dorff protested.

"I'll see to it she isn't. Just you be prepared to move the moment she comes into view." Rawlings drew down a walnut writing desk recessed into the back of the front seat. He placed Ford's manuscript on the desk and began to read, concentrating totally on the job at hand, his eyes traversing each line of the penciled manuscript, skipping nothing.

Absently he drew a ball point pen from his pocket and made an occasional note on a pad of paper: a name, a place, a page number, all this while barely taking his eyes from the manuscript before him. Occasionally he turned back to an earlier page to corroborate a reference ... and then jotted another note on the pad. At one point he was aware of a voice asking him if he'd like a cup of tea or a sandwich; Wernicke was going out. Rawlings shook his head no. He was dimly aware of Wernicke leaving the car and returning, and of the rustle and tear of paper as the sandwiches were unwrapped, and of the sounds of satisfaction the men made as they sipped their hot tea.

Somewhere he heard Dorff ask what he was finding of such great interest there. "A treasure map," Rawlings breathed without looking up. "A veritable treasure map."

It was twelve-thirty by the clock on the dashboard. The street was filling with office workers hurrying to and from their lunches. Rawlings didn't see or hear them. Dorff's voice, exploding in his ear, broke his concentration at last. "There she is now."

She was across the street in front of the hotel, searching through her purse for proper change for the cab. Rawlings quickly tucked the manuscript back into the envelope and handed it to Dorff. It was as if he had not been lost in another world for the past two and a half hours.

Casey turned from the cab and started for the hotel as

Dorff left the car. "I'll see to it you have time," Rawlings said. "But don't waste it." As Dorff hurried across the street, Rawlings lifted the car phone and placed a call. Dorff was already entering the hotel just behind Casey.

"Hotel Cardigan," came the voice of the switchboard operator.

"Would you page Mrs. Casey Ford, please? I believe she's in the lobby."

"One moment, sir."

Rawlings could hear the operator's voice echoing back from the lobby loudspeakers: "Telephone for Mrs. Ford. Will Mrs. Ford come to the lobby phones, please?"

Rawlings handed the car phone to Wernicke. "When she comes on ask her to hold for a moment for—ah—Mr. Price-Jones."

"Who in hell is Mr. Price-Jones?"

"Who in hell knows. She'll hold on for a moment just to find out. When you hear my voice coming over the line from the hotel you can hang up."

Rawlings slipped out of the car and crossed the street. He went in through the revolving door, his eyes making a sweep of the lobby. He saw Casey approach the desk and take the phone from the clerk. Elevators were to the left. Casey must have been on her way to the elevators when she heard her name announced. Stairway beside the elevator bank. Dorff must be on his way up those stairs now. The far end of the lobby, in a direct line that would take him past Casey, opened into a bar and grill room.

He saw a look of consternation and puzzlement cross Casey's face as she listened to the voice on the phone. Wernicke must just have asked her to please wait for Mr. Price-Jones to come on. Why was it, he wondered, that people would wait for a call from a person with whom they were not at all acquainted? He removed his hat, unbuttoned his coat, and made directly for the grill room at the far end of the lobby. He would pass directly behind Casey.

Casey began shifting impatiently from foot to foot. She turned and leaned against the desk, her elbow supporting the forearm that pressed the phone to her ear. Dorff, Rawlings thought, would be approaching her room about now. Rawlings passed within a yard of Casey, but she was looking the other way. He had hoped she would see him coming. Rawlings stopped, turned, and took two tentative steps toward her. She sensed a presence close behind her and turned. They were almost directly face to face, their bodies almost touching. Her expression of annoyance at having to wait for the mysterious Mr. Price-Jones gave way to puzzlement and then to startled surprise. Her hand, holding the phone, dropped to her side. Rawlings could hear Wernicke's voice filtering through the earpiece: "Sorry for the delay. He'll be just one more moment, Mrs. Ford." Poor Wernicke. Casey must have been threatening to hang up.

Casey's jaw went slack and she gulped down a breath. And her voice came out, thin and high pitched with astonishment as she spoke his name. "Eric!"

Rawlings smiled, delighted. "It *is* you. I couldn't believe my eyes . . ." He heard the click in the phone as Wernicke broke the connection.

Casey looked flustered and glanced across his shoulder at a mirrored pillar nearby to check her appearance. Her cheeks felt hot and she was afraid she was blushing.

"But it's amazing how little you've changed," Eric said.

"Only where it doesn't show," Casey answered lightly, "at least not with my coat on." She felt like an ass as soon as the words were out. But what do you say to a man you haven't seen in twenty years? She noticed the deep rills bracketing his mouth, and his eyes had a strained, steely look she didn't recall from the past. She became aware of the telephone dangling in her hand and brought it up to her ear again. She listened for a moment and realized the line was dead. "Hung up on me."

"I hope it wasn't important."

"I haven't the slightest idea what it was," she said cheerfully and dropped the receiver into its cradle. "If it's really important he'll call again."

"You're here on business, I suppose?"

"Why, yes. How did you guess?"

"No one in his right mind would come here in the dead of winter for pleasure. Publishing, isn't it?"

"You're not in publishing, too?"

"Far from it, I'm afraid."

"Then, how did you know? Editors are a fairly anonymous bunch, except to the trade. Don't tell me you're with C.I.D. and have a dossier on me."

Rawlings laughed. "Nothing so mysterious as that. I've seen Charles periodically over the years. He's kept me up-to-date on you."

Casey's face darkened. "Charles is dead, you know."

Rawlings managed a look of astonishment, dismay. "I didn't know."

Casey nodded. "In Salisbury. Just a few days ago."

"I didn't know. I've been out of the country. What happened?"

"An accident." She chose not to go into the details.

"I'm dreadfully sorry, Casey."

"Yes." She shrugged, as if that gesture would shake off the dark knowledge that weighed on her like a cloak of lead. "Well, you knew Charles. It might have been predicted that he wouldn't die a natural death."

"He had a great fondness for you, Casey, despite . . . everything."

"No need to make excuses for the past . . . for any of us. Maybe Charles was just ahead of his time . . . in that way, at least. Nowadays the type of ménage he set up for the three of us on that ship has become so commonplace nobody gives it a second thought. It's supposed to be therapeutic."

"Perhaps it is now. In the context of our time, it certainly wasn't." Rawlings caught a glimpse of Dorff moving through the revolving door out into the street. "Casey, I have to get on to a business appointment. Will you be in London awhile?"

"Three more days."

"Perhaps we could get together and talk. Lunch? Dinner? Are you free this evening?"

"Dinner tonight would be very nice."

"Suppose I come by at six-thirty?" He held out his hand. She took it. "You have no idea how pleased I am to see you again, Casey."

Casey nodded and thought wryly, time is a healer all right, and a sleight-of-hand artist, too. I feel as if I'd seen him only yesterday, but all the fires are out. He's just a friendly face in a foreign land.

Rawlings winked, turned and started out of the lobby. And only then, as she watched his retreating figure, did she notice with dismay the stiff, swinging gait of his ruined left leg. She had to restrain herself from running after him. Some healer! she thought soberly, some magician! is our friend Father Time.

RAWLINGS EASED HIMSELF into the back seat of the car beside Dorff and tapped Wernicke on the shoulder. The Bentley slipped away from the curb and melted into the flow of traffic. "Everything all right?" Rawlings asked Dorff.

"Done," Dorff replied. "Smooth as glass."

"Not quite yet. I need a copy of that manuscript. When we get back to the flat I want you to phone around to the copying firms. Find one that will stay open for a special job tonight between seven and nine. That should give them enough time to Xerox about a hundred pages. We'll pay them whatever extra charges are incurred for the overtime."

"What if she's in her room this evening?"

"She won't be."

"How can you be sure?"

"Because I'm taking her to dinner."

Wernicke half turned his head in astonishment. He almost ran the car into a pedestrian island.

16 ***

AT FOUR-THIRTY that afternoon Casey sat soaking in her bath, sipping a bourbon highball, giving herself up to the balmy embrace of the water and the tranquilizing effect of the drink. Objectively she took stock of herself as she thought about her dinner date with Rawlings. The years hadn't been unkind to her. Her legs were still lithe and firm. Her breasts, always large for a frame as slender as hers had once been, floated roundly, buoyed up by the water, looking almost like a girl's. She knew that was an illusion. Time and gravity had taken their toll on that part of her anatomy.

She sipped her drink and considered the day. It had been a very good one. She had come to a handshake agreement with a British publisher for the American rights to a promising first novel. She had spent a pleasant afternoon with the author at his flat in Chelsea discussing the book and some minor changes she hoped he would make for the American edition. And, of course, there had been the meeting with Eric in the lobby. How very nice that had been. He would be coming for her in just two hours' time. She felt very young, very feminine. She would leave the bath in a little while and take a short nap and look positively radiant when Eric came. Perhaps she had deceived herself before. Perhaps the intervening years had not completely erased the past. Perhaps he was more than just a friendly face in a foreign land. She put her drink down on the ledge and slid deeper into the tub and watched her breasts bob. Vanity, she thought. You are not without vanity. Why were you so pleased that he recognized you? Was it because it meant that you had somehow confounded time? You still looked enough like the girl you had been to be identifiable to someone who knew you then and had not seen you since? And why should that matter? But it did.

Her cozy mood was broken by the ringing of the phone on the night table beside her bed. She cursed mildly, set her drink down on the tub rim and stood up, dripping. She grabbed a towel off the rack, stepped out of the tub, and sighed as she caught a glimpse of herself in the full-length mirror on the door, her belly and her breasts becoming victims of gravity again. By the time she got to the phone the line was dead. The phone had rung only twice. The operator came on with, "Did you wish to place a call?"

"No," Casey replied, annoyed. "I just had a call."

"Your caller disconnected."

"Was there any message?"

"No, mum."

Casey hung up the phone wondering if it might not have been the mysterious Mr. Price-Jones again or, her insecurity returning, Eric calling to cancel their date. But surely he'd have let it ring more than twice. She felt all on edge again, the calming effect of the bath fading as her feeling and look of youth had faded when she stood up in the tub.

She went back into the bathroom and opened the drain. Then she finished drying herself, replaced the towel on the rack, picked up her drink, and sat down in the easy chair near her bed. She wondered if Eric had been genuinely happy to see her or whether he might not have seen in his fortuitous meeting with her the means to some end. Perhaps he was as down at the heels as Charles had been. Insecurity swept through her like a dark wave churning up silted-over memories of how she had been used in the past. Suddenly the sight of Charles' manuscript in its manila folder on top of the pile of other manuscripts offended her. She crossed the room and put it into a drawer out of sight. She didn't want to think about it. But the harder she tried to think of other things, the more her mind returned to the manuscript and to a page in it that had been gnawing at her consciousness all day. It was just a few paragraphs, really, in which the protagonist finds in a notary's safekeeping a message from his vanished family. There was the notary's name, Hoff-something-or-other, and a street in Amsterdam.

She swallowed the rest of her drink, slammed down her glass, crossed to the bureau and angrily pulled open the drawer. She took the manuscript out of the envelope and found the page. Masterhoff was the name. Jan Masterhoff, a notary in the Herengracht.

She glanced over at her travel alarm clock. She would have an hour until Eric came for her. To hell with her beauty rest. She wasn't all that beautiful and she'd get precious little rest with this thing troubling her mind. There was a way of testing her theory about Charles' story. She could check out the veracity of this part of it at least. The question remained, did she really want to?

Want to or not, she had to.

She picked up the telephone and waited for the circuit to open.

When the operator came on Casey shut her eyes like a child faced with bad medicine. Then she poured out her request in a rush, afraid that if she paused once for breath she would be unable to continue. The party's name was Masterhoff. His office was in the Herengracht. In Amsterdam. In Holland. They would have to try to get his phone number through information. Was it possible to do that?

"We'll try," the businesslike operator replied. "Please hang up, now. I'll ring you back in any case."

Casey dropped the receiver back into its cradle and took a deep breath. Her heart was racing. She went to the closet and slipped into her robe. She lit a cigarette, went to the window and drew the drapes aside a crack, looking out across St. Martin's Lane, her mind carrying her beyond the North Sea to a street in Amsterdam that might or might not exist . . . to a man named Masterhoff, who might or might not be. And, if there was such man, might Charles merely have lifted his name out of a phone book as some authors were inclined to do? Or was it possible that he could be holding for safekeeping an envelope belonging to Charles . . . addressed to her?

She crushed out her cigarette and lay back on the bed, and fidgeted, and got up again. She might as well start dressing. She went into the bathroom where her stockings and bras hung drying on a nylon line. The bras were still damp. She took down a pair of stockings and carried them back into the bedroom and found a clean bra in the bureau drawer. She slipped out of her robe and dropped it onto a chair. The phone rang.

Casey crossed the room apprehensively, half hoping the operator had found Masterhoff's number, half hoping that Masterhoff didn't exist. She picked up the receiver.

"This is the operator, Miss Ford. Sorry about the delay. We're ringing your number now."

"Masterhoff. *Mag ik u helpen?*" He sounded old and cross.

"*Mijnheer* Masterhoff?" She didn't know why she used *mijnheer* instead of Mr., since she couldn't speak another word in his language.

"*Ja. Ik stond op het punt mijn kantoor te verlaten.*"

"Do . . . you . . . speak . . . English, *Mijnheer* Masterhoff?" she asked, spacing out her words and enunciating very clearly.

"Of course." It was heavily accented English. But it was English. "But who is this I am speaking to? It is after business hours you must realize. I was already out the door when the phone began to ring."

"I'm terribly sorry, *Mijnheer* Masterhoff. But I'm calling from London and I'll only be a moment."

"How may I be of assistance to you, then?" Masterhoff sounded resigned. He was probably uncomfortably buttoned up in his overcoat in an overheated office.

"I have been trying to locate . . . a friend. I had reason to believe he might be . . . a client of yours."

"Who, please?"

Casey took a deep breath. "A Mr. Charles Ford."

"I'm afraid, no. I have no such client." Masterhoff had barely stopped to think. He must have his clients' names tucked away in his head as in a Rolodex file.

Casey sighed, not certain whether she was relieved or disappointed. Charles *had* fabricated the whole thing. He must have just plucked Masterhoff's name out of a phone book to fit a character in his story. "Thank you, *Mijnheer* Masterhoff. I'm sorry to have troubled you."

"One moment, please." Masterhoff stopped her. "May I ask to whom I am speaking?"

"*Mrs.* Ford." She was using the "Mrs." a lot these days, she thought.

"One moment, please." He didn't sound annoyed or grumpy anymore, but businesslike and alert. She heard a dull thunk as the phone was set down on the desk. He was back thirty seconds later. "May I ask your first name, Mrs. Ford?"

"Casey. Why?"

*** **78**

"Beginning with a 'C' as in—ah—cable?"

"Yes."

"Tell me, please, if you will, Mrs. Ford. Have you a middle name?"

Her apprehension began to dissipate. "Why, no. I'm afraid not."

"You do not sign your name with a middle initial?"

The dark wave swept back through her. "Why, yes. But that's my maiden name. Rafferty."

"Casey R. Ford?"

"Yes." She was beginning to feel weak around the knees. This man she had never met or heard of, except as a name in Charles' manuscript, knew something about her.

"Ah!" He exhaled with satisfaction. "I thought the name Ford registered when you mentioned it."

"But you said you had no such client."

"I have not!" he replied firmly, as if his integrity had been questioned. "But I have an envelope for *you,* Mrs. Ford."

"Left by whom, may I ask?"

"A client."

"May I ask this client's name?"

"I am not at liberty to say."

"Would you be so kind as to forward the envelope to me, *Mijnheer?*"

"I am afraid that would not be possible. My instructions were that I was to hand it you in person upon verifying your signature."

"But you don't have my signature, *Mijnheer.*"

"But I do. My client has left me a sample of your signature."

"When may I come?"

"Any day at your convenience. You will find me here

between the hours of nine and twelve-thirty. I go home for lunch and return at two o'clock until five-thirty. You will, of course, in addition to your signature, bring the letter of authorization."

"Letter?"

"I cannot turn over the envelope without both your signature *and* the letter of authorization."

"Letter?" Casey asked again, dumbly, panic clawing at her.

"You have it with you, I hope?"

And then she knew. She shuffled through the manuscript until she found the page where, in Charles' own hand was part of a letter of authorization, the one that was supposedly found in the rubble of the childhood home of the protagonist in his story.

"Yes," she said. "Yes! I think I have it," her excitement growing. Her mind now synchronized with Charles'. The letter had been placed in the manuscript by design. The manuscript had been written in longhand by design, so that the letter in Charles' own hand would seem part of the whole. The entire camouflage job had been carefully worked out. And then, her mind racing ahead, she asked: "*Mijnheer* . . . actually I have only part of the letter. The name of the addressee and the salutation have been torn away."

"Exactly," said Masterhoff. "The upper part has been left in my care. The two halves must form a whole."

Casey did some fast mental juggling. She could postpone her afternoon appointment in London tomorrow, fly to Amsterdam, and be back in the evening. "May I come tomorrow?"

"As I have said, any day at your convenience, between the hours of nine and twelve-thirty, and two and five-thirty."

"Thank you, *mijnheer*."

*** **80**

"My pleasure, *mevrouw*."

She hung up, her heart racing. She was too agitated to lie down again, too excited to dress. Her hands were clammy. She paced the room, smoking, thinking, wondering.

She wished she had thought to ask Masterhoff the size and bulk of the envelope. It might have been the size of an ordinary mailing envelope or as big as a briefcase and stuffed with valuables or money. She thought she might try ringing his office again, but he would surely be gone by now. Even were he there she doubted he would discuss details over the phone with someone whom he had identified only tentatively. She glanced at her clock on the bureau. She had damn well better start getting dressed. Eric would be calling for her soon. She made a final adjustment on her girdle and began fitting herself into her brassiere, mentally damning all the paraphernalia with which civilization had saddled womankind. Who had decreed that a woman would fall apart without the structural support of girdles, bras, garter belts, and armpit shields? No medieval knight had ridden into battle more encumbered with hardware.

She wondered if she should discuss Charles' manuscript and Masterhoff's mysterious envelope with Eric. Eric had known Charles, had been a friend of his at one time, had kept up an acquaintanceship with him over the years. She felt she had to talk to someone about it or she would burst. And then she decided she'd better talk to no one, not until she'd seen the contents of that envelope in Masterhoff's keeping. It might be perfectly harmless, or it might be a matter for the police. Whatever it was, Charles had entrusted it to her. Better keep Eric out of it, for now at least.

Finally encased in the whole compendium of undergarments, she went to the bathroom, ducked under the clothes drying on the nylon line, and confronted herself in the mirror. She picked up a comb and began pulling it through her hair. The business of the signature puzzled her. She wondered where Charles had gotten the sample he'd left with Masterhoff. He couldn't have clipped it off one of the letters she'd sent him because she'd always signed those simply, "Casey." There were the occasional loans she'd made him by personal check. Those were signed with her full name, "Casey R. Ford." Charles must have traced her signature from one of those checks onto a card . . . or learned to forge it freehand. Was Charles capable of such deviousness? Casey smiled wryly. Charles was capable of . . . anything.

The telephone rang again. This time it was Eric calling from the lobby.

"Shall I come up for you?" he asked brightly.

"Not unless you're prepared to pick up where we left off almost twenty years ago. I haven't finished dressing yet."

"Hmm." Eric considered a moment.

"Never mind," Casey said quickly. "I'll be down in ten minutes."

"I'll be waiting."

"Eric," she asked, troubled by a thought. "Did you call between four-thirty and five?"

"No. Why?"

"I just wondered. Somebody phoned and hung up when I lifted the phone. I guess it was a wrong number."

17

ERIC PUT DOWN THE HOUSE PHONE and crossed the lobby to the grill room where Dorff had taken up a position at the bar that afforded him a view of the elevators and the stairway. "There'll be a ten-minute delay," he told Dorff. "She's dressing." Dorff nodded and sipped his drink. "I'll ring you up at the copying house when we've finished dinner. If the job's done and you've left, I'll bring her back to the hotel. As an extra precaution, I'll have Wernicke ring her room from the car when I bring her into the lobby, just in case you're still up there, though there's no reason why you should be. That'll give you time to clear out. I don't want any surprise meetings between the two of you. I don't want any accidents. She is *not* Ford. I'm quite sure she's totally unaware of his activitics."

The bartender was approaching, an expectant, business-like smile on his face. "I want to impress that fact on you," Rawlings said to Dorff. "In a way she has been his victim as much as any of us have."

"What'll it be, sir?" the bartender asked brightly.

"I'm afraid I haven't time, now," Eric apologized. He slipped down off the stool and walked out into the lobby. The bartender followed him with his eyes, his cheerful countenance crumbling. Then he turned to Dorff and, as if to compensate for his having lost one customer, asked, "Will you have another, sir?"

"Just the bill, please. I'll have to be leaving any minute now."

OUT IN THE LOBBY, Eric took one of the free travel-tips pamphlets off the rack on the hall porter's desk and found an empty lounge chair across from the elevator. He turned the pages of the pamphlet without really seeing them, nagged by troubling thoughts. Dorff was a professional, thorough and efficient. He could be trusted. But he had been conditioned by life to reflex action in emergency situations, the deed almost preceding the thought when it came to self-preservation. Eric could not really condemn this quality in Dorff. Indeed, he was indebted to whoever had made Dorff what he was. Dorff had saved his life at least once and brought him safely through more than one tight situation. Dorff had done this because it was part of his job, not because of any great fondness for Rawlings. Indeed there had always existed a kind of guarded animosity between the two men. They worked together from time to time because their skills were complementary. But neither really liked the other. Their temperaments were too opposite.

He glanced into the grill room. Dorff was sitting where he had left him, an empty glass in front of him, waiting.

He wished that Casey had not stumbled into this affair. Personal feelings had no place in his business. They reduced one's operating efficiency. Seeing her again, at a time in his life when he was beginning to question the validity of the pursuits which had been the foundation of his existence for so many years, was particularly unsettling. Despite the sordidness of the way in which they had met so long ago, this spirited girl, a woman now, represented one of the few human relationships that had touched him. She

*** 84

belonged to that time when he had been relatively unsoiled. In a way he had become as much a machine as Dorff, as loathsome as Ford. He had spent his youth and entered middle age with blinders on, in single-minded pursuit of the bank accounts of men long dead, the money-lined vaults of ghosts. To this end he had debased himself in the company of Ford and a dozen others like him over the years. He detested the Fords of the world, yet he had used people as ruthlessly and as wantonly as they had . . . and for what?

The elevator door opened and Casey stepped out, glanced quickly around the lobby and caught his eye as he rose to meet her. Her pugnacious lower lip stretched into a grin, and her eyes were bright and merry as she moved quickly toward him with her coltish loping gait.

She hasn't changed at all, he thought. But then, neither have I . . . on the surface.

Outside the hotel, he guided her to the waiting Bentley. She stopped in front of the liveried chauffeur holding open the door and stared at Rawlings in disbelief. He gave her a gentle, encouraging nudge and assured her the car wasn't stolen.

She hesitated before getting in. "I've never ridden in one of these before."

Eric smiled and helped her in. "It requires no special training. If you don't get carsick in a taxicab, you qualify." He turned to Wernicke before following Casey into the car. "We'll go to The Barge."

"Yes, sir," said Wernicke as he shut the door with a juicy thunk.

"What sort of business are you in, anyway?" Casey asked as she ran her hands over the rich glove leather of the seats.

Eric shrugged. "You might call it banking. International banking."

Wernicke got in behind the wheel and the car moved soundlessly into the flow of traffic.

18 ***

THE BENTLEY DREW UP at a Thames-side pier below Chelsea, beside a barge fitted out with a superstructure like a houseboat, its haloed lights glowing dimly behind a screen of evening mist.

"What's this?" Casey asked.

"The Barge."

"It looks positively sinister."

"That's one of its main attractions."

"You're sure I'm not about to be shanghaied?"

"If you are, you'll be in the most exclusive company. Your ordinary run-of-the-mill shanghaiees couldn't raise the price of the coat check here."

Casey looked uneasily across at The Barge as Wernicke popped open the door on her side and waited for her to step out. "Very posh, huh?" she asked dubiously.

"Royalty has dined here."

"Did you say dined or died?"

"Then you *have* tasted the food!" Eric said with mock accusation.

"No." Casey laughed. "I've never set foot in the place in my life."

"Wait 'til you get inside." Eric followed her out of the car, took her arm and guided her to the angled gangplank which rose and fell with the swell of the river. She heard a thunk behind her as Wernicke shut the car door.

"I wonder how many customers they've lost just going in and out on that board?" she asked.

"Who knows?" Eric replied lightly. "They issue no casualty reports; rule of the house. It would discourage business. But trust me, you'll find it absolutely charming."

"Just as long as I'm not susceptible to seasickness, right?"

"Right."

The door was opened for them by a grizzled fellow dressed in the bell-bottomed trousers and peppermint-striped blouse of a nineteenth-century seaman. He looked surly and menacing, and Casey muttered under her breath to Eric, "Are you sure we're in the right place?"

"Of course. He's one of the reasons the lords and ladies of the realm love to come here. He spices up their humdrum lives with the illusion of danger. They certainly don't come for the food, although that's pretty dangerous stuff, too: old-fashioned English cooking."

"I don't know why English cooking is so maligned," Casey protested. "I don't think I've ever had a really lousy meal in London."

"That's because you're here on business and you're wined and dined in continental-type restaurants. Any Englishman with a really cultivated palate and the pocketbook to support it flies to Paris for dinner."

They checked their coats, and Eric took her by the arm again and led her to the bar. "Actually I've just brought you here to have a look at the place and a drink. We'll go to the Minotaur for food."

The bar was a long, rough board laid over six large kegs. The barstools were smaller kegs.

Casey ran her palm across the top of one of the stools before venturing to sit down.

"Don't worry," Eric assured her, "there are no splinters. It's very carefully sanded."

"The royal seat, huh?"

"Exactly."

"I suppose," she mused, sitting down, "that not even the nobility is so bored it'll risk its ass for local color."

Eric laughed and sat down beside her.

The dining area was in a well between the bar and a raised platform across the room. The tables were packed with customers dressed in a variety of costumes, ranging from designer gowns to tie-dyed jeans, from tuxedoes to turtlenecks. An accordion trio mounted the platform at the other end of the room and began playing a medley of old sea chanteys.

"Can't we eat here?" Casey asked. "I'd really like to see what honest English cooking is like."

"It's a lot like old shoe leather. But I'll see if we can get a table." He signaled for the maitre d'. A bulbous-nosed boatswain with a mottled red face came to them in answer to Eric's signal. Yes. They might have a table for two, but there would be a thirty-minute wait.

"Do they allow dancing while waiting?" Casey asked after the maitre d' had departed.

"They allow just about anything," Eric replied. "It's one of the attractions of the place. But," he patted his crippled knee, "I'm afraid I don't do the hornpipe anymore."

"I'm sorry," Casey said contritely. "I'd forgotten. How did it happen?"

"A riding accident," Rawlings lied breezily. "I've had little luck with horses and women."

"Oh! I don't know about that." Casey winked. "You always seemed pretty good in the saddle to me."

Eric laughed. A waiter dressed as a cabin boy went past carrying a tray of food to one of the tables. Casey inhaled. "That certainly *smells* delicious."

"What you're smelling is all the flavor that's been cooked out of it. It's all in the air, not in the dish." He took note of Casey's empty glass. "Another?" he asked.

"Why not? If it's really as horrid as you say, I might as well anesthetize my palate."

Eric ordered another round of drinks.

"Tell me," Casey asked, "you saw Charles occasionally over the years . . ."

Eric gave her a guarded look. "Yes . . ."

"Have you any idea what he was up to in all that time?"

"You corresponded with him. What did he tell you?" Eric responded evasively.

"All kinds of things, most of which were hard to believe. He claimed he was in real estate at one point. A development project in the Algarve in Portugal. Another time he was selling mutual funds to American servicemen attached to NATO. There were a dozen different schemes, all of them sure shots. But each letter ended with a pitch for a loan of anywhere from a hundred to several hundred dollars to carry him through until the payoff."

"He never returned the money, I suppose?"

Casey shook her head no. "Did he borrow from you, too?"

"Yes. And perhaps from a number of other people. I know I helped him out three or four times, although he never paid back any of the money."

"He was like a man at a slot machine. He kept chucking everything he had into it, plus whatever he could con out of soft touches like you and me. He seemed so sure that if he kept at it long enough he would hit the jackpot."

"But where was the money going? Do you suppose there ever was a real-estate project in the Algarve?" Eric asked, leading her.

*** 90

"Maybe he was just biding his time . . . using the money to sustain himself."

"For what?"

"For some big payoff . . . somewhere. You know what wealth meant to him. I think at one point he may have begun to live a kind of fantasy. He began to believe that there was a fortune held in trust for him somewhere."

Eric toyed with his drink, avoiding her eyes. "Did he ever mention anything about this . . . hidden wealth directly to you?"

"No . . . not exactly."

"Then what would make you think of it?" He prodded her gently, attempting to find out what she knew or surmised, careful not to reveal that he knew everything she knew, and much more.

"He had begun to write a book. It was a very strange book, an attempt at a novel, but not really a novel. To someone who didn't know him intimately, it would appear to be a piece of fiction, a kind of grotesque fairy tale. But I spotted things in it that read almost like a diary in spite of the camouflage. It was in there, in his book, this business of treasure waiting to be claimed."

"I agree with you," Eric said abruptly; "he had begun to fantasize, poor chap. It really is very sad."

"That's what I thought, too, Eric, at first. I told you that. But truthfully, I'm not so sure. Charles wasn't a creative writer. He might have been capable of putting down the story of his own life . . . but I don't think he could have written a sustained piece of fiction."

"But you're contradicting yourself," Eric said, trying to reverse her line of reasoning. "You just told me that this story of his, if it is indeed autobiographical, is so camouflaged as to appear to be a fairy tale. That indicates a gift for fiction. After all, for a con artist like Charles almost any undertaking is a kind of fiction. Look at it another way. If there was, indeed, some treasure waiting for him, why did he spend all those years scrounging, borrowing, begging?"

"Well . . . according to his story . . . he didn't know precisely where it was until the man who had amassed it died."

"You mean one of those deathbed revelations."

"According to Charles' story."

"Fiction, Casey, fiction," Rawlings said lightly, deprecatingly.

"And then the location was inaccessible for a number of years after that," Casey continued dejectedly. She wished she hadn't opened up on the subject, and decided to drop it. She certainly wasn't going to bring up the business of Masterhoff in Amsterdam. Charles had bequeathed her a problem. It wasn't in her nature to saddle Eric with part of the burden. "I may just drop the whole matter in the laps of the police," she said, hoping to change the subject.

"Oh, dear!" Rawlings laughed. "You don't want to do that, not if you're here to transact business. They'll have you tied up for weeks. If you do decide to drop it in their laps, wait until your business is done and you're back home in your own country. After all, it's not an emergency. That money, if it does exist, has been lying around for a generation. It can certainly wait a few weeks longer."

The accordion trio finished its set; the three musicians put their instruments down on their stools and stepped off the platform. They passed through the restaurant to their dressing rooms to almost no applause.

Eric stared thoughtfully at his drink, considering how best to begin a new line of questioning without making it appear more than just casual conversation. Finally he asked,

"Tell me, Casey. In his letters to you, did Charles ever mention a partner in any of these undertakings of his?"

Casey smiled sardonically. "He never mentioned anyone but himself. Typically Charles, don't you think? He never even mentioned that he'd seen you from time to time. That I do find strange."

"Oh . . . perhaps not so strange . . . considering everything. Anyway, it would be, as you say, typically Charles not to."

"*Did* he have a partner?" Casey asked. Short of actually involving Eric, she was determined to arrive at Masterhoff's armed with as much knowledge of Charles' activities as she could gather. And Eric began to wonder who was questioning whom.

"My dear, I assure you, I was no more privy to his secrets than you."

"I know. It's just that he might have mentioned something in conversation that he wouldn't have troubled to put into a letter, especially a letter devoted to equal parts boasting and begging for a handout."

"Well, I don't see that matters much now, do you?"

"Maybe. Maybe not."

"Why maybe?"

Casey looked troubled. "Because . . . in that manuscript of his there is a partner mentioned . . . or, rather, a shadowy figure who once was a partner of sorts."

"A partner in what?" Eric asked lightly, trying to mask his alarm over how much Casey had learned from that manuscript. Rawlings was well aware of Ford's aborted partnership, would have been aware of it had he never seen Ford's manuscript. He had lived Ford's story too, and knew most of the details by heart . . . except those few elusive vital details that would end his search. He was almost

93 *

certain, now, that the manuscript would provide him with those.

"I don't really think I want to go into all that," Casey was saying. "But I have a feeling, from what I read, that this partner was not welcome from the beginning. He forced himself on Charles, a kind of blackmail. In Charles' story, he finally cuts the partner out, double-crosses him, plain and simple, although Charles didn't word it quite that way, and in turn is pursued by the partner and . . ."

"And what?" Eric encouraged her to continue.

Why not, she decided. Eric Rawlings was a friend to them both. "Eric, if that story of his has more truth in it than fiction, then . . . perhaps the reason he died was very different from the way it looked to the police."

"I'm sure it *must* be fiction," Eric assured her. "I think you're more disturbed by Charles' passing than you let on. I think you're letting your imagination run away with you. You and I are both aware of certain sexual proclivities of his. His ending the way he did was probably inevitable. I'm sorry, Casey. But in the light of his history, I think the police came to exactly the right conclusions."

"And his manuscript?"

"I haven't read it, of course. But from what you tell me . . . a fantasy. Absolutely. If it has a ring of truth to it in your eyes, perhaps that is because, in a sense, his life itself was a fantasy."

Casey sighed. "Perhaps you're right." But she knew he wasn't. She had spoken to Masterhoff in Amsterdam.

Eric patted the back of her hand. "No 'perhaps' about it. I *am* right. For your own sake you must believe that. Don't pick up where Charles left off, chasing after phantoms."

"I can't even publish it," Casey said despairingly. "It has no ending."

*** 94

"Perhaps it's better that way."

The headwaiter in the boatswain's uniform signaled to them. They picked up their drinks and followed him to their table. The accordion trio threaded its way back through the restaurant, stepped up onto the platform, and began another set of songs.

19 ***

DORFF GOT OUT OF THE MOLDED PLASTIC CHAIR and shambled over to the counter where one of the technicians was standing, holding the phone out to him, and loudly calling his name. The monotonous buzz and thunk of the Xerox machine had so numbed his eardrums and filled his skull over the past hour that he hadn't heard the phone ring. Bright emerald rectangles pulsated rhythmically behind his eyeballs, the reflection of the green strobe light that flashed with each page that was photographed. He wondered how the technicians took this assault on their senses hour after hour, day after day, without going deaf, blind, or mad. He plugged one ear with the little finger of his left hand and pressed the phone against his right ear with the other hand.

"Dorff," he shouted into the mouthpiece.

"Rawlings here. Are you about done?"

"In more ways than you can imagine. I've lived through artillery barrages that have proved less unpleasant. They're about done now."

"Good. We'll be leaving in a few minutes. Will half an hour give you enough time to get the original back in place and clear out?"

"A half-hour should do it."

"Good. We'll take a short motor tour before returning to the hotel. Then I'll have Wernicke ring the room from the car after I've brought her into the lobby . . . just to make certain you're out of there. If you're still there and you hear the phone ring, clear out."

Dorff turned his back to the Xerox machines and cupped his hand around his lips and the mouthpiece so that there was no chance of being overheard. "Is she on to anything, do you think?"

"I think she may be. But she doesn't know quite what she's on to. Nothing to worry about at the moment."

"Oh?" Dorff asked. "And when do we start to worry, when she and Ives are off somewhere dividing up the booty?"

"She has nothing to do with either Ives or the late Mr. Ford in this matter," Rawlings said firmly.

"I wonder."

"Don't. It's not your forte."

"I hope your judgment isn't being colored by your feelings."

"I want you out of that room before she arrives."

"I think you're making a mistake."

"Leave the thinking to me. *Do I make myself clear?*"

"You do," Dorff replied resentfully. "But you made one mistake in trusting Ives. I think you're making another one now."

"Then I'll have to answer for it. But if you act against my wishes in this, you'll answer for it . . . to me. Clear?"

"Clear," Dorff replied grudgingly.

"We'll be waiting in the car to pick you up across from the hotel in St. Martin's Lane." Rawlings hung up.

Dorff slammed down the phone and turned to the man operating the Xerox machine. "Is it going to take you the bloody rest of the night to finish up those last bloody pages?" he shouted.

Five minutes later Dorff was down in the street, his coat

97 ***

collar turned up against the cold, flagging down a cab. He carried two thick manila envelopes under his arm. One contained Ford's original manuscript, the other contained the copy. He had the cab stop first at Rawlings' flat and wait while he dashed out and left the copy with the porter. Then he got back into the cab and gave the driver the hotel's address. He sat back, thinking bitterly that something would have to be done about Rawlings after this job was over. The man was growing soft.

Fifteen minutes later, in Brewer Street, a quarter of a mile from the hotel, Dorff rapped sharply on the screen separating the back seat from the driver. "What the bloody hell is going on?" he yelled. The cab had been stopped for what seemed an interminable length of time. They were halfway down the block, with stopped cars lined up ahead and behind, firmly locked into a hopeless traffic jam.

"Sorry, sir," the driver apologized, "there seems to be a dustman's lorry working up ahead. We'll just have to wait 'til they move on."

Dorff rolled down the window and stuck his head out the side. He could see the dustmen now, working at the curb near the next corner. "How the hell long do you suppose they're going to be blocking this street up?"

"Can't be more than a few minutes. I'm truly sorry, sir."

Dorff looked around. The drivers behind him had begun honking their horns, but none of them seemed to have the good sense to back out of the street.

"There ought to be a law," Dorff growled, as he reached into his pocket, peering over the driver's shoulder at the meter.

"Just a few minutes, sir," the driver assured him.

"I haven't got a few minutes." He thrust the fare at the driver and thrust himself out of the cab. He jogged ponderously down to the corner, past the lorry, and looked about wildly for another free cab. Then he decided the hell with it. It was only six blocks to the hotel. It might take him as long to find a cab as it would to go it on foot. He set out at a brisk pace, just short of a trot.

Dorff arrived in the hotel lobby eight minutes later, breathing hard. He made directly for the elevators, saw that they were both moving up toward the higher floors, cursed under his breath, and started for the stairs.

20 ***

ALBERT CORNING WAS DISTRESSED. The day had been a long series of frustrations. First he had discovered that Casey Ford had not registered at the Charing Cross. Then he had spent most of the afternoon going methodically through the phone books, patiently ringing hotel after hotel, asking to speak to her. It had not been until four-thirty that he had gotten a positive response from the Cardigan. Now, having finally gained entry to her room, he had come up with zero for his effort. He tilted his tweed hat back on his head and surveyed the room again. He had been through every drawer, every suitcase, every closet. He had examined the piles of manuscripts on the desk and searched the pockets of all the clothes on their hangers. And he had found nothing. This did not in any way diminish his conviction that Charles Ford had left something behind and that whatever it was, it was in Casey Ford's possession. She had, in her interview with him at the Wild Boar Inn, mentioned a manuscript, and that manuscript was nowhere to be found. Perhaps she had lied about it, made it up, in order to cover the true nature of the contents of the package she had received in Salisbury. Whatever was in that package, she was either carrying it with her now . . . or she had already passed it on to some other interested party.

The jangle of the phone startled him, sending adrenalin coursing through his system as if another person had suddenly appeared in the room. He picked up the phone and listened. Perhaps the woman had an ally. Perhaps the caller was that ally. Perhaps he would identify himself in some way before he realized that he was not speaking to Casey Ford.

But the message was brief, anonymous, and oddly pertinent. "Clear out. She's on her way in." There was a click as the connection was broken at the other end.

"Thanks, chum, whoever you are," Corning said into the dead mouthpiece and dropped the receiver back into its cradle. He moved quickly to the door, glanced around to make certain that everything was as it had been when he'd entered the room, and let himself out, listening for the click as the lock-tongue snapped into place. He heard hurried footsteps thudding on the carpet around the corner of the corridor and wondered if it could possibly be Mrs. Ford already. And he wondered who had warned him off a moment ago. He took three quick steps in the direction away from the oncoming footfalls and let himself into the public lavatory diagonally across the hall. He made a quick check and found the stalls unoccupied. Then he returned to the door and eased it open a crack.

There was a man, a hulking figure, standing casually in front of Mrs. Ford's door, as if waiting for someone to answer his knock. In his left hand he carried a large manila envelope, the parcel from Salisbury. To the eye of a casual observer he might have appeared perfectly innocent and commendably patient. But Corning noticed that he was standing inordinately close to the door, and that his right arm was making short, jerky movements as he neatly slipped the lock.

Gingerly, silently, Corning eased the lavatory door shut. Corning knew that hulking profile; it was engraved on his

101 ***

consciousness. And the knowledge that Dorff and therefore the whole rotten wolf pack had somehow gotten one step ahead of him added a new element of urgency to his mission as well as a new set of hazards. He wondered, too, whether Dorff and company might have established an alliance with Mrs. Ford. But no. From the manner in which Dorff was attempting to enter the room, Corning reasoned, they were probably working *around* her.

Corning eased the lavatory door open a crack again, watching for Dorff to leave. Instead he saw Casey Ford, loping down the corridor, her purse slung over her shoulder. She stopped in front of her door and opened the purse, hunting for a key. There was a shadow of a smile about her lips and she seemed to be humming a tune.

Inside Casey's room, Dorff counted down three from the top in the stack of manuscripts on the desk and slipped Ford's envelope into the place from which it had been taken. As he turned, he caught sight, through the open bathroom door, of the stockings and brassieres hanging invitingly on the line. Damned women, he thought, leaving things like that hanging about for anyone to see. He had seen them two hours before when he had come to take the manuscript away, when the room had still been redolent of Casey's perfume. The sight and smell, coupled with his memory of the silhouette he had seen in the window in Salisbury, had stirred him. He hadn't had a woman in over a week.

He ventured into the bathroom, cupped one of the pendulant brassieres into the palm of his hand and nuzzled it. Disappointingly, it had been freshly washed. No scent remained of the woman who had worn it. He took one of the stockings down and ran it through his fingers, fleshing it out in his mind with the recollection of Casey's long coltish legs. His erotic reverie was interrupted by the startling rattle of a key turning in the lock of the hall door. He spun around and stood frozen for a moment, transfixed by the sight of the door swinging open.

Bloody imbeciles, he thought, they said they'd ring up and warn me. Instinctively, he twisted the stocking between his hands, turning it into a weapon, if needed, a garrotte. And then Casey Ford was standing in the open doorway, staring wide-eyed into the bathroom.

Dorff tensed, ready to spring, watching the woman's mouth open, knowing he couldn't reach her before the scream came. And then, to his astonishment, her expression changed from defenseless bewilderment to outrage. Instead of a scream the open mouth gave voice to an angry demand. "Who the hell are *you?*"

Dorff shrugged, looked about as if dazed, tried to disarm her with a pretense of helplessness and confusion, moving toward her all the time, desperately trying to get within reach of the door, within reach of escape.

"Get your ass out of my room before I call the . . ." She stopped in mid-sentence, her eyes for the first time catching sight of the silken garrotte spanning the gap between Dorff's outstretched, importuning hands. He had forgotten it himself. And now Casey's outrage metamorphosed into fright. Dorff saw where she was looking and let one end of the stocking fall, spreading his hands apologetically. But it was too late. Now the scream would come. Dorff was burly, but he wasn't slow. He hurled himself across the short distance that separated him from Casey and the door, his right hand outstretched, ramrodding into the door, slamming it shut; his left hand cupped, falling over her mouth, covering half her face.

For a moment they both stood, pinned to the door,

103 *****

stunned, his body blanketing hers. Then he abruptly crumpled in on himself, grunting like a poleaxed bear as she drove her knee up into his groin.

Casey slipped out from under him as his grip on her relaxed. He was bent over double clutching his belly, grunting and sucking in air. He couldn't hold onto her, but she couldn't get out of the room. He had sagged against the door, his great weight blocking her exit.

Dorff grimaced hideously as he strained to straighten up. He watched Casey's frightened eyes move from the door to the telephone on the desk across the room. As she backed away from him and around the bed he strained against the knots of pain in his belly, heaved himself upright, and stumbled after her, falling on her at the desk, pinning her hand to the phone with one mammoth paw so that she couldn't lift the receiver. Gasping, sapped of power, he used his bulk and weight to hold her immobile until the pain subsided.

Beneath this sweaty, suffocating canopy Casey was growing faint with fear. She shifted her foot until she felt it come to rest on his. Then she raised her heel and, summoning her last reserve of strength, brought it smashing down onto his instep.

Dorff howled and recoiled, and Casey slipped free. It was her last chance. She knew as she stumbled toward the door that, whoever he was and whatever he had been doing in her room, he would kill her now if he managed to lay hands on her again. She could hear him moving after her as she fumbled with the knob and pulled the door open . . . and found her exit blocked by another bear of a man looming in the doorway.

*** 104

21 ***

FIRST THERE WAS A SOUND of breaking glass and then there was a scream. Rawlings glanced up in time to see what looked like an explosion in a window on the sixth floor; a disintegrating pane of glass bursting from its frame, flying shards and a hurtling shape, a rain of crystal and a tumbling figure in billowing clothes. Rawlings shut his eyes before the body hit. But he couldn't shut his ears. Even a half block away he could hear the horrid hollow smashed-melon thump as the body struck the pavement.

He stood immobile beside the Bentley, trembling, his eyes still shut, his ears still echoing with the sound. His fists were clenched so tight that his manicured nails were cutting into his palms. A hand gripped his shoulder. He turned and found himself confronted by Wernicke's pale face. "He's killed her," Rawlings rasped through clenched teeth.

"I warned him she was on the way up," Wernicke shot back defensively. "Why didn't he get out?"

"I'll kill him," Rawlings gasped. "He knew she had nothing to do with this affair. I'll kill him."

"Let's clear out of here," Wernicke pleaded. He opened the door to the Bentley and tried to help Rawlings in.

"We'll wait! I want to be here when he comes out."

"You're not making sense. It might have been an accident."

"Of course it was. Dorff's specialty is accidents."

"Get in the car . . . please. What's done is done. There's too much at stake."

"I'm sick," Rawlings muttered. "I'm sick of it all." All the strength seemed to drain out of him. He sagged against the fender of the Bentley. Wernicke took Rawlings' arm again, and this time Rawlings let him help him into the car.

"We'll go now," Wernicke said softly.

Rawlings shook his head. "We'll wait for Dorff."

Wernicke closed the car door, as if by this act he could keep Rawlings from harming himself or Dorff. He stood beside the car like a sentinel, not sure whether he was standing there as a beacon for Dorff or to warn him away. Halfway down the block a crowd had already formed around the body on the sidewalk. A man burst out of the crowd, looking up and down the street and then began running in Wernicke's direction.

Wernicke tensed as the stranger sprinted toward him until he realized that the man's eyes weren't on him at all but on the bright red public phone booth on the corner a few paces beyond. The man plunged into the phone booth, yanked the receiver from its hook and began dialing the emergency number. It was a simple number, only three digits, nine-nine-nine, but he was so distraught his finger kept slipping and he had to try two or three times before he got through.

"An ambulance, quick!" he shouted. "Cardigan hotel. Poor soul just threw himself out the window." The man repeated the name of the hotel, his voice rising and cracking with hysteria.

Wernicke stared at him for a moment, trying to digest what he had just overheard. Then he bent down and looked through the window of the car. Rawlings was sitting rigidly in his seat, staring straight ahead with unblinking eyes, his jaw locked tight, the muscles along the jawbone twitching spasmodically. Wernicke left the car and walked quickly down the street to where the mob had gathered. He worked his way through the crowd until he stood at its inner rim. He looked down at the broken figure sprawled on the pavement.

One arm was flung out as if reaching for some invisible support. The other arm was crushed beneath the body. A rivulet of blood, already thickening in the icy night air, ran like a grotesque tongue from the broken mouth to the cold concrete. Wernicke wondered why the man who had run up the street to the phone booth had done so with such urgency. Dorff was beyond help. He must have been dead the instant he hit the sidewalk.

Wernicke worked his way back out of the crowd and walked quickly toward the car. The man who'd placed the call was out of the phone booth, pacing back and forth on the corner, looking anxiously about, waiting to direct the ambulance he had just summoned.

Wernicke slipped into the driver's seat of the Bentley and turned around to face Rawlings. "Eric," Wernicke said with fearsome intensity, trying to get Rawlings' attention. Rawlings continued staring straight ahead, his jaw twitching, his nostrils flared. "Eric!" Wernicke repeated. "You must listen to what I am about to say." If Rawlings heard Wernicke he gave no sign. "Eric," Wernicke tried again. "The woman isn't dead."

Rawlings' eyes shifted to the right, piercing Wernicke with a murderous and distrustful look.

"That's Dorff lying out there on the street. It's Dorff," Wernicke repeated, "not the woman."

"Are you certain?" The voice was flat, dry, threatening.

"I went down there myself and saw the body."

107 ***

"You're sure it wasn't Casey?"

"For God's sake, Eric, I can tell the difference between Dorff and a woman. It was Dorff."

There was a raucous hooting of sirens and a kaleidoscopic flashing of lights as a police car, followed by an ambulance, came skidding around the corner. The man who had placed the phone call went running past the Bentley down the street in pursuit of the two speeding vehicles. The ambulance door swung open and an attendant leaped down, reached in, and drew out a rolled stretcher. The policeman opened an aisle for him through the circle of onlookers. The circle closed in like quicksand, engulfing the policemen and the ambulance attendants.

Rawlings watched, waiting for them to bring the stretcher out, waiting to confirm what Wernicke had told him.

"They could be there half the night," Wernicke pleaded. Rawlings didn't answer.

A policeman came out of the crowd, trotted up to the corner near the Bentley and began diverting traffic from the street.

Rawlings opened the car door.

"Where are you going?" Wernicke asked nervously.

"Wait here. I'll be right back."

Rawlings got out of the car, pulled his coat collar up around his chin and walked the few paces to the corner. He called out to the policeman directing traffic, "What seems to be the trouble?"

"Bloke just took a dive from the sixth floor," the policeman called back.

Rawlings nodded and returned to the car. He shut the door and sagged against the cushion. "Let's go," he said to Wernicke. He was very tired.

He would finish this job, he promised himself, and then

*** **108**

he would pack it in. Something had gone out of him completely. He had felt it going for some time. But this incident had pulled the plug. He was so glad it was Dorff and not Casey. He would finish this job and then he would vanish. He had forgotten how to hate. He could give his life no more to settling old accounts.

Wernicke started the engine and tapped the horn to attract the attention of the policeman at the corner just behind him. He motioned that he would like to back out. The policeman nodded and held traffic on the main thoroughfare while Wernicke put the car into reverse and eased out around the corner and out of the street.

Driving to Rawlings' flat, Wernicke asked, "What do you suppose went wrong?"

"I don't know," Rawlings replied.

"You don't suppose *she* could have shoved him?" Wernicke asked.

Rawlings shook his head. All he could feel was relief that it was Dorff and not Casey lying in the street.

"You don't suppose he heard her at the door and tried to hide outside on the ledge?" Wernicke asked.

Rawlings shook his head. "He went right through the window. I saw the flying glass."

"Then what happened?"

"I don't know."

"Do you think it might have been Ives? Could Ives have been up there . . . waiting?"

"For what? Ives is way ahead of us. What could he have wanted up there?"

"Maybe he's not as far ahead of us as we think. Maybe Ford didn't tell him everything he needed to know. Maybe there was a missing piece he's looking for. But how could Ives have managed to overpower Dorff?"

109 *

Wernicke was a good man, Rawlings was thinking, he had a mind. He wished Wernicke had been with him the past six months instead of Dorff.

"Perhaps he surprised him."

"What?" Rawlings asked distractedly.

"I said perhaps Ives surprised Dorff. He would have had some advantage then."

"Perhaps."

"You don't sound convinced."

"I don't know. I'm wrung out."

"Shall I book us another flight?"

"No. We'll leave tonight as we planned. If you're right about Ives we certainly can't afford to delay."

When they got back to the flat Rawlings found the envelope that Dorff had left for him. At least the poor bugger had done something right. Rawlings changed his clothes, packed his bags, and then, with Wernicke's question about Ives still troubling him, he rang Casey's hotel room. If Ives had indeed sent Dorff out the window he must have been in the room at about the same time Casey was arriving. He might have harmed Casey, too.

Somebody picked up the phone at the other end. And that was a relief. "Casey?" Rawlings said.

"Detective Sergeant Hartigan here. Who's this?"

"I'd like to speak to Mrs. Ford, please."

"So would we," Sergeant Hartigan replied. "Mrs. Ford hasn't returned to her room. Perhaps you'd care to leave your name?"

Not on your life, Rawlings thought as he hung up. Rawlings crossed to the window and stared out. If Casey wasn't in her room, where was she?

*** 110

22 ***

CASEY WAS IN THE BACK SEAT of a cab speeding down the road to Heathrow airport, past the dark shapes of low suburban houses, their windows aglow like jack-o'-lanterns' eyes. She sat perfectly still, her purse on her lap, her hands folded on her purse, her eyes cast down on her hands. She was still numb with shock. Corning sat beside her, watching her anxiously.

Thirty minutes before, he had manifested himself like a slab of granite in the doorway of her room, blocking her exit as Dorff came lurching toward her. For one terrifying moment she stood trapped between the two hulking men. Then she lay sprawled on the floor, dazed, a phantasmagoria unfolding around her as Corning stopped Dorff's lunging, head-down charge with a lid-lifting kick to the jaw. Swinging his right hand like an ax blade, he chopped Dorff back across the room with slanting blows to the face and side of the head. Had there been a wall to block Dorff's stumbling retreat he would have crashed back against it and crumpled to the floor. But there was no wall. There was only a window, and it offered no resistance.

Corning picked up the manila envelope from the desk and Casey's purse from the floor. He checked the purse to make sure her passport was inside, then he thrust the purse into her hand. He found the room key lying on the floor. He used it to lock the door after them, leaving Casey's luggage and spare clothing behind. The room was left as if she hadn't returned to it that night.

He took her by the arm and led her, stunned and unprotesting, to the elevator. Downstairs, he dropped her key into the slot at the reception desk. She remained immobile, as if she were in a trance. Then he led her out the front door and in the opposite direction from the side street into which Dorff had fallen. A block away Corning hailed a cab and told the driver to take them to Heathrow airport.

His great concern was that she would come out of her state of shock at the airport, or on the plane, or while clearing customs, and, like a sleepwalker suddenly awakened, become hysterical, unmanageable. Still, there was no other way. It was a chance he would have to take. He needed her help. He needed her with him, on his side.

"You're not a police officer, are you?" Casey asked suddenly, emotionlessly, in a soft monotone.

Good, he thought, she's coming out of it. Better here than elsewhere. "No," he replied, "I'm not." There was no point in continuing the Inspector Corning masquerade. A police officer wouldn't be fleeing the country with a woman he had just rescued from a homicidal burglar.

"I've known since Salisbury that you weren't," Casey sighed.

"You didn't turn me in to them, I hope." He said it lightly, as if it were a joke, trying to camouflage his alarm.

"How do you mean?"

"Offer up a description, ask for a warrant for my arrest, that kind of thing."

"No. I just phoned the station house to speak to you about a matter that occurred to me after you'd questioned me. They said they had nobody there by your name. Then I knew."

*** **112**

"And you pursued it no further?"

"Perhaps I should have, but I didn't. I wasn't ready to, yet."

"This . . . matter you wanted to speak about . . . did it have anything to do with the parcel Ford left you?"

Casey nodded.

"Perhaps you'd tell me about it once we're settled."

Casey nodded. "Perhaps. I owe you something. But first I'll want to know who you are, Mr. Corning."

"I'll explain that too, once we're settled. It won't be long. Just a little patience. Until then I only ask you to trust me."

"I suppose I can do that. You did save my life." She was still stunned and bewildered, accepting any hand that might help her.

Corning relaxed, easing back into the seat as the cab approached the perimeter of the airport.

They got out of the cab and Casey walked with Corning from ticket counter to ticket counter until he found an airline with a plane ready to depart and two available seats. He would have gone to Paris or Rome or Istanbul, the destination didn't matter. The important thing was to get himself and Casey out of the country before the exits were closed. He bought two tickets on a Sabena flight for Brussels.

23

WHEN THE PLANE WAS AIRBORNE and arcing southward through the night across the Channel, Corning opened the manila envelope and bent over the pages on his lap, reading quickly and avariciously. Casey watched him in silence, a trace of ironic amusement on her face. After a while he turned to her, puzzled and distraught. "Is this the package they gave you in Salisbury?"

Casey nodded.

"But it's just a story."

Casey nodded. "I've already told you that."

"Then why did Dorff want it bad enough to risk his neck for it?"

Casey shrugged.

Angrily Corning turned the pages, not really reading them, just looking for something, anything that might be hidden between the sheets of paper, as if the manuscript might be one of those old books with a hiding place cut out in the middle. Finally, despairingly, he riffled through the pages, like a blackjack dealer running his thumb through a deck of cards. Something caught his eye. He stopped, glanced at Casey. Her face was a mask. Greedily he turned back through the pages, beginning at the end of the manuscript, searching . . . until he found the page that had eluded him, the incomplete letter. He read it carefully, then turned to Casey again. "This is it, isn't it?"

Casey shrugged disinterestedly.

"Don't play games with me, Mrs. Ford," Corning snapped, the air of gentle interrogation of Salisbury gone, as was the solicitousness of the drive in the cab from London. Corning was a bloodhound who had just picked up a scent.

"Mr. Corning," Casey said, "if that is your name, I owe you something for saving my life back at the hotel. But I don't know who you are, or what this is really all about. I'm not sure I even know why Charles left that manuscript behind for me, since it's apparent now that the last thing in the world he would have wanted was that it be published. Until I know what this is all about, I will aid neither you nor anyone else. In fact, when this plane lands in Brussels I intend to turn around, take the next flight back to London, and get what help I can from the police. I'm only sorry now that I didn't do that yesterday."

Corning studied her gravely for a moment. He squared off the pages of the manuscript and slipped them back into the envelope. Then he sighed. When he spoke again his manner was as gentle and solicitous as it had been in Salisbury and in the cab.

"Mrs. Ford," he said, "when I first approached you in Salisbury I was attempting to find out what I needed to know without involving you. I was trying to spare you. When I came to your room in London I was pursuing that same course, but you were in trouble and I felt compelled to step in, and now, unhappily, you *are* involved. And, since you now seem to have recovered from the shock of the . . . incident, I will, since you insist, tell you the whole story. When I'm through I hope you will choose to help me, for I'm sure you know I can't stop you from asking for the police when we leave this airplane. But, if you call in the police, you must know it will be very bad for me. And, as you said before, you do owe me something."

"I don't think you should be concerned about the police,

115 *

Mr. Corning. I would make it very clear to them that what you did was done in self-defense . . . or, rather, my defense."

"There's more at stake than that, Mrs. Ford. I can only hope you'll understand that when I've finished saying what I have to say." Corning glanced at his wristwatch. They had been in flight for twenty-five minutes. Another thirty minutes was all the time he had to make his case. He had no idea what this woman's political or ideological beliefs might be. He could only hope that his appraisal of her as a woman of compassion, a woman with a sense of justice, was correct. He had not really known any people in the arts, but it was his impression that they tended to be humanists. He took another moment to organize his thoughts. Then he began.

"Mrs. Ford . . . let me start with a question. How much do you know, actually know, of your husband's background? I don't mean his recent activities. I mean ancient history: his family, his origins, his childhood, his youth."

Casey looked puzzled by this question, but she told him what she knew. "He was a war refugee. His parents were Czech. They sent him to England in 1939. I think he had relatives there. I believe an aunt had married an Englishman named Ford. He took their name. He couldn't have been more than a child, maybe thirteen or fourteen. Toward the end of the war he joined one of the exile army units. He fought with them in the final push across Europe. He emigrated to America after the war."

Corning nodded, but there was a bitter twist to his mouth. "Yes! That was the saga of Charles Ford. Poignant. Impressive. He made capital of it for most of his adult life. And it was a lie. It was, in fact, almost directly the opposite of the truth . . . except that he was, in a sense, displaced by the war and did eventually go to America."

*** **116**

Casey stared at him uncomprehendingly. "Did you know Charles?"

"Yes. In a way. I knew him intimately, though I never actually met him personally. I have lived with his face before my eyes and his real history and that of his family engraved on my memory since the end of the war. You might say he was my life's work, my vocation, my obsession.

"But, before I go on, let me confirm what you already have surmised. My name is not Albert Corning any more than his name was Ford. But . . . Albert Corning must serve, for the time being at least. Now, let me tell you something about myself." He paused and tugged the sleeve of his jacket up until it was almost at his elbow. Then he unbuttoned his cuff and rolled his shirtsleeve up over his forearm. He held his arm out for Casey to see. "My credentials," he said.

Casey stared down at the tiny blue numerals tattooed above his wrist.

"You have seen one of these before?" Corning asked.

"No," Casey said softly. "But I've read about them. Concentration camp."

Corning nodded. "Bergen-Belsen."

"I'm sorry."

"Nothing for you to be sorry about. You had nothing to do with it. But Ford's father did. Karl Fautz was his name. It was Ford's name too, before he changed it. But there were no relatives in England, not true relatives, anyway. There was a childless married couple named Ford. They were of middle age and English by birth. But they were Hitler sympathizers. They were sleepers in the pay of the Abwehr. They had been enlisted in 1937, long before the outbreak of hostilities, and their duties were simple. They were to remain dormant, pursuing their normal lives until

117 ***

called upon to act, most probably at the time of the invasion. There were sleeper cells like this seeded throughout Britain in the years before the war. In 1939 this couple took under their wing a young refugee boy from Czechoslovakia. This was the one you would come to know as Charles Ford. But he was no Czech and he was no refugee. He was a member of the Kriegkind, the war children, a select group of German youth chosen to join the sleeper cells in England, to mature there, and to take on the more strenuous assignments in the event of a protracted war. Throughout England, these sleeper families were infused with fresh young blood in this manner.

"Your husband was perhaps not ideally equipped for this duty. Even as a boy he was small and lacking in physical strength and courage. But Karl Fautz, his true father, pressed for his acceptance into the corps. Fautz felt that in this way his son would be shielded from the eventual hazard of shouldering arms and facing the enemy in open combat."

"Who was Karl Fautz to have been able to secure such favors for his son?" Casey asked.

"Not a very big fish. He was a dentist by profession, in Lübeck. He was also an opportunist and a man who knew which way the wind was blowing. He was an early booster of Hitler. Eventually he became a member of the SS. He also knew how to look out for number one. In the closing years of the war, when others were freezing in the East or being chewed up by Patton's tanks in the West, he arranged to be assigned to duty in the relative safety of a concentration camp. There he worked with a colleague, another specialist in the field of oral hygiene. Fautz and his colleague were responsible for extracting gold teeth and inlays from the jaws of the corpses before they were sent into the ovens. It must have been back-breaking work. There were, in those last years of the war, as the Reich was collapsing, so many corpses, so many teeth. Have you any idea how much gold might be mined from so many hundreds of thousands of mouths?"

Casey shuddered.

"Suffice it to say," Corning continued, "the sum would run into the millions. But in this undertaking Fautz and his colleague were not totally honest. For every two or three ounces of gold delivered to the Reich, they kept one for themselves. They took their share out, hidden on their persons, a few ounces at a time, until by the time the war ended they had a fortune secreted away in caches in the countryside, hiding places known only to them. They made a pact that, when the war ended, they would divide the proceeds equally. Or, if only one of them survived, half the money would be turned over to the heir of the other.

"Fautz' colleague was killed in the final collapse of the Reich. Perhaps he died at the hands of the enemy. Perhaps he died at the hands of Fautz. Fautz survived.

"He acquired false papers and a new identity and vanished into the confusion of displaced humanity. He may have fled to South America, but he eventually returned to Europe. It can be surmised he was trying to find some way to reclaim the treasure he had buried."

"Why didn't he take it out with him at the end of the war?"

"He didn't dare. The concentration camp in which he had served and the countryside in which he had secreted the hoard had fallen into the Soviet sphere. It wasn't until recently that businessmen and tourists could travel back and forth across those borders with relative ease.

"He died here in Europe a few years ago, but not before

119 *

he had been reunited with his son and not before he revealed the location of the treasure to him. You may have wondered why your husband spent so many years leading a gypsy life. This is why. He knew of the treasure. And he knew his father was alive somewhere. He spent those years making contacts, attempting to reopen closed channels, retrace forgotten escape routes. Eventually he succeeded."

Casey was neither claustrophobic nor a hysteric. But suddenly the airplane seemed tight and hot and strangulating. She swallowed back a rising nausea. She fought to maintain her equanimity. But the feeling that she had befouled herself through her marriage was overwhelming.

"How is it that you are so certain of all this, Mr. Corning?"

"As I told you, Charles Ford and that gold have been my life's work. I will tell you a little about myself now, Mrs. Ford. After the war, after I was released from the camp, I joined a group of fellow victims dedicated to ferreting out those criminals who had escaped . . . finding them and seeing to it that they received the punishment that was their due. Part of this work included locating the fruits of their plunder and using it to make reparations to their victims. Perhaps you've heard of the Phoenix Bureau?"

Casey nodded. "Yes. You're the group that found von Loder in Paraguay about six months ago. It was in the papers in America."

"Von Loder and Pfizer and Müller. The list is long, and it still isn't ended."

"But why spend all that time pursuing Charles? He was guilty of nothing but being his father's son."

"I quite agree. But the gold did not belong to him any more than it belonged to his father. It was not Charles

Ford we pursued but the gold. Six or eight months ago we began to suspect that at last he was bringing it out . . ."

"Did Charles have a partner in this business?" Casey asked, startling Corning.

Corning looked up, wary. "What would lead you to think so?"

"It was hinted at in a roundabout way."

"By whom?" Corning asked.

"A man you wouldn't know."

"His name?" Corning insisted.

"Rawlings. Eric Rawlings."

"You have spoken to Rawlings?" he asked, thoroughly discomposed.

"He's an old . . . acquaintance. I knew him years ago. I met him again in London, just by chance."

"And he told you about this business of the gold?" Corning asked, patently alarmed.

"No. He told me only that he'd seen Charles over the years and that he suspected lately that he had been engaged in certain illicit activities . . . petty smuggling, he thought it was."

"And *he* told you that Ford had a partner in this . . . smuggling activity?" Corning was trying to suppress his agitation. "What else did he tell you about this . . . smuggling? And this . . . partner?"

"That's all. It was just a social evening. And we were discussing Charles, among other things."

"And what did you tell him?"

"What could I tell him? I knew nothing of any of this."

"You had this manuscript. Did you mention it?"

"I mentioned the manuscript."

"Did you go into detail?"

"No."

"Why not?"

"I chose not to. Why does it matter?"

Corning bit his lip and squeezed the bridge of his nose with his forefinger and thumb. He seemed to be in a state of great distress. He thought a moment, then took a deep breath and said, "Let me finish the story about Fautz. Something I left out because I felt it irrelevant as far as you were concerned. But now it has become of utmost importance. You remember I told you that Fautz had a confederate who was killed in the last days of the war . . ."

"That couldn't have been Eric. He's Charles' age or younger."

"No. Of course not. Your mutual friend, this . . . Mr. Rawlings, is the son of Fautz' SS confederate. This . . . Rawlings," he almost spat the name, "was also in the Kriegkind in England. But Ford was gutless and Rawlings was dedicated. In the closing days of the war the Kriegkind was given the signal to activate, to do what it could to damage the British war effort by sabotage. Ford, like his father, read the direction of the wind and lay low. Rawlings attempted to do his duty and was captured and imprisoned. With the end of hostilities, Ford fled to America to escape the retribution of those members of the Kriegkind who served and suffered the consequences. He remained in America on a student visa . . . until he felt it safe to return to Europe. He knew about the gold. But he didn't know where it was hidden, nor did he know where his father had gone into hiding.

"Rawlings knew of the treasure, too. But since *his* father had perished, the only way he could claim his rightful share was to find Ford and apply leverage to persuade him to agree to an alliance."

"Charles' manuscript hints at blackmail."

*** 122

"Perhaps that was the lever."

"Then . . . Charles and Eric were partners in this?" Casey asked incredulously.

"Uneasy partners. Yes. When Ford's father was finally located and the secret given up, Ford and Rawlings worked together to bring the gold out of Eastern Europe, a little bit at a time, over a period of almost two years."

"Then Eric has the gold," Casey said, recalling the Bentley and his apparently opulent way of life.

"No," Corning replied. "Nobody has the gold . . . yet. Last year Rawlings returned to Eastern Europe to bring out the last of the cache. He was taken into custody by the police. Someone had placed an anonymous call to the border patrol."

"Charles?"

"Of course. Apparently he hoped that his partner would remain in prison for a number of years, at least. He remained there for months, not years. But by that time Ford had moved the gold again. Now Ford is dead. And your Mr. Rawlings is determined to find the gold. So am I." He patted the manila envelope. "My hope is that you will help me to decipher *this*."

Casey was speechless. Corning's revelations had shaken her, and left her profoundly disturbed. She needed time to absorb what she had just heard and come to terms with herself in the light of her former feelings about two men who had loomed large in her life. And there was Corning, sitting beside her in the cramped airplane cabin, waiting for an answer.

"But you have no more right to that gold than Charles or Eric," she blurted, startling herself by voicing aloud a question that had only been a thought in the back of her mind.

123 ***

"Perhaps so," Corning replied quietly. "Rightfully it belongs to those from whom it was stolen. But they are dead. And we are their living arm of retribution. We must have that money to continue our work. I believe, if the dead could speak, they would tell you that they want it so. I ask again, will you help?"

CASEY MADE NO PROTEST as she and Corning cleared customs at the Brussels airport. Nor did she make inquiry about the return flight to London. She felt an obligation to help Corning in his quest, to make up in some way for the unwitting assistance she had given Charles over the years in his pursuit of his father's plunder. She felt compelled, too, to see where Charles' story would lead her. Her business contacts would simply have to accept her apologies and her explanations when she returned. They owed her that for a lifetime of unfailing punctuality. She waited while Corning exchanged a number of English pounds for Belgian francs. Then they got into a cab and Corning asked the driver to take them to any good hotel in the center of town. If Casey weren't too fatigued they could sift through the manuscript tonight and be prepared to make their next move in the morning. Casey replied that she thought it would be better if they got a decent night's sleep since she already knew what their next move should be. She told Corning about her telephone call to the notary in Amsterdam.

The taxi stopped in front of the Hotel Arcadia opposite the Bourse. Corning paid the driver and hurried with Casey into the lobby.

At the reception desk his first inquiry was not about the availability of rooms, but about the first direct train or airline service to Amsterdam in the morning. The clerk was nonplussed but obliging. He drew several railroad and airline schedules out from a shelf under the desk and patiently ran his fingers down the columns of departure times.

Casey opened her coat and fanned herself with the lapels. If the British were averse to central heating, the Belgians seemed to be just the opposite. The lobby felt as hot and dry as a sauna.

The clerk finished his perusal of the schedule. "O nine hundred," he said.

"Rail or air?" Corning asked.

"Rail. But from here to Amsterdam it matters little. The trip is only two hours by train, direct to the center of the city."

"Have you two single rooms for the night?" Corning asked.

The clerk looked a little surprised at the request, but replied with a sigh, "In Brussels in March we always have rooms. Have you baggage?"

"Lost in transit," Corning lied. "You know the airlines."

The clerk nodded sympathetically and said, "You will have to pay for the rooms in advance, then. A thousand francs."

Corning counted out a thousand francs. The clerk handed him the registration cards and made note of their passport numbers while Corning and Casey signed in. The clerk rang for the bellboy.

"No luggage?" the bellboy asked.

"The airlines." The clerk shrugged.

The bellboy led them to the elevators. He didn't seem to know what to do with his hands without luggage in them.

125 *

"I'm afraid you'll have to sleep in your clothes," Corning apologized to Casey.

"Not if the rooms are as overheated as the lobby, I won't," Casey replied, as the elevator door slid shut.

24 ***

THEY ARRIVED IN AMSTERDAM at eleven-twenty and hurried from the chilly sepulchre of Central Station into the tight, warm cocoon of a waiting taxi. They sat silent and tense in the back seat as the cab sped them up the Damrak, along the canal through the center of town, past clusters of glass-domed sight-seeing boats laid up at their moorings in tarpaulin shrouds. Winter-stripped elms lined the roadway like forlorn sentries, dark with winter, denuded of leaves, sheathed in transparent coats of ice. Casey was overcome by a feeling of pity for these sad, naked trees; the same unaccountable pity she sometimes felt for statues in the park on freezing days.

They crossed cobblestoned Dam Square, circling past the blue-windowed countenance of the Hotel Krasnapolsky, and followed the tram lines until they came to the Herengracht. There they crossed the short humpbacked bridge over the canal and followed the street along the waterway past orderly rows of narrow, gabled houses that served as office buildings, consulates, and headquarters for manufacturers and exporters whose business arms reached around the world.

Masterhoff's building belonged to no single corporation or country but was parceled out in individual suites to a dozen small, independent professional men and entrepreneurs.

Corning paid the driver and helped Casey from the cab.

He glanced at his watch as they started across the sidewalk. It was eleven-thirty.

"What time did you say he left for lunch?" Corning asked.

"Twelve-thirty."

"Good." Corning pushed open the glass and wrought iron outer door. The vestibule was a narrow whitewashed rectangle, immaculately clean, with an inlaid parquet floor, highly polished, and a thick mat set just inside the door for visitors to wipe their feet on. Black and white nameplates on a row of brass mailboxes on the left-hand wall listed the occupants and their office numbers. Masterhoff was 4-B. There was no call or buzzer system in evidence.

Corning opened the inner door. It let them into a narrow hallway, narrower than the vestibule, the parquet flooring showing on either side of a narrow gray carpet running the length of the building. The steep stairway, also carpeted, was on the right. There was no elevator.

"It looks like we'll have to climb," Corning said.

"That's all right, I've got good legs."

"I'd noticed," Corning said.

At the foot of the stairs Casey stopped Corning. She opened the envelope containing the manuscript, found the page that served as a letter of introduction and took it out. "Here," she said, handing Corning the manuscript, "hold on to this a minute." She tucked the "letter" into her purse. "I don't think it's necessary for Masterhoff to know that the letter is part of a larger work."

The fourth floor hallway was a duplicate of the first floor, narrow, parqueted, protected by gray carpet. There were two doors facing the hallway. Masterhoff's, 4-B, was at the rear.

Corning's knock was answered by a muffled grunt that might or might not have been an invitation to enter. He tried the knob and the door opened.

The room—for Masterhoff's office was just one room— was large and well lighted by a window that ran almost from floor to ceiling at the back of the house. The wall behind Masterhoff's desk was lined with shelves stacked with heavy legal volumes and ledgers. A row of six tall steel file cabinets was set against the wall opposite the window. Masterhoff was sitting behind his desk in the center of the room, a jolly-looking fellow, pink-faced and portly, with bushy white eyebrows and a halo of white hair ringing his otherwise bald dome. He didn't rise to greet them but rather wriggled a little in his chair. He seemed at first to be grinning, an inordinately wide and white-toothed grin.

One step into the room and Casey realized the wide grin was a white handkerchief tied across his mouth and knotted somewhere behind his head. Several yards of clothesline wrapped around his chest pinned him to the chair. His hands were tied to the armrests, his ankles tied to the legs of the desk. He grunted again and wriggled again to indicate that he was alive and would like some help.

Casey ran to Masterhoff while Corning coolly took time to close the door.

"I can't get this damned knot untied," Casey muttered. Corning crossed to her, digging in his pocket. He came up with a gravity knife and expertly flicked open the blade.

"Hold still a moment," he ordered the squirming Masterhoff, as he prepared to slip the blade under the gag. "I don't want to cut your ears off by mistake."

Masterhoff went rigid, and Corning sliced through the

gag with a single stroke of the knife. No sawing away at the cloth. The blade was razor sharp.

"*Dank u wel*," Masterhoff gasped. "*Ik heb dorst*."

"I'm afraid we don't speak Dutch, *Mijnheer*."

Masterhoff switched to English. "I said, 'thank you.' I thought I would die of thirst." Casey poured a few ounces of water from the carafe on the desk into a glass and held it to Masterhoff's mouth. He drank greedily, coughing and dribbling the liquid over his shirt-front, while Corning cut the ropes binding his chest, arms, and ankles. As soon as his arms were free, Masterhoff reached for the carafe and poured a few more ounces into his glass.

"What an adventure. Is that the right word?" He sounded hoarsely exuberant as he tossed down the contents of the glass. "No use trying to call the police on that phone. They've torn the cord from the wall." His breath was beginning to smell like a barroom around closing time. Casey looked at him and at the carafe.

"*Jenever*," he explained. "I have found it helps keep the chill away on these cold winter days."

"Who did this?" Corning demanded.

"Ah! If I only knew. He was wearing a ski mask. Very smooth, very professional, just like in the cinema. He was most efficient and most gentle. I never felt really threatened —is that the proper word?—even though he did have a pistol." He poured some more gin from the carafe. "You'll have to excuse me, perhaps I am somewhat unnerved. I'll go down the hall in a minute and inform the police, although I doubt it will be of any benefit. I can't give a description. If you would care for a drink I have another tumbler in the cabinet over there."

"What did they take?" Corning asked intensely.

"They? I told you there was just one man. Of course,

there might have been another in the hallway. A lookout, eh? Is that the proper word? But I would have no way of knowing."

"What did *he* take?" Corning asked again with impatience approaching anger.

Masterhoff's bright blue eyes darted from Corning to Casey and then back to Corning again. "I am beginning to have a feeling that we are victims here of a most unfortunate accident of timing." He looked at Casey again. "Would you, by chance, be the lady who phoned me last evening? Mrs. Ford?"

Casey nodded, opened her purse, and took out Charles Ford's letter. Masterhoff glanced at it and waved it away. He swiveled his chair so that he was facing away from them, facing the window. Corning rudely spun the chair back. Masterhoff looked deflated and frightened.

"What did they take?" Corning snapped. His fists were clenched. Casey placed a restraining hand on his arm.

"Please," she said firmly, "he's an old man."

"He's a bloody chicken-livered boozehound. I wouldn't be surprised if he traded it to them for a case of gin."

Masterhoff sat there, with his elbow on the arm of the chair and his forehead resting in his palm. He looked so crushed and dejected that Casey was moved to comfort him. She knelt and patted the stubby, gnarled hand that rested on his knee. There was a sound of metal drawers being drawn open and slammed shut.

"It's all right. It was unavoidable," Casey said softly.

Masterhoff began to babble, all his early bravura gone. "You don't understand. I am not what he says. I am a responsible man. But I am not equipped for . . . this. I was frightened. I was so frightened I . . . I . . . "

"They got it!" Corning's voice cut through Masterhoff's

131 ***

mutterings. "The bastards got it." He came back from the cabinets holding an empty manila file folder labeled FORSTER-FORD. "The bloody fool here had it all neatly set up in alphabetical order. A child could have found it."

Masterhoff snapped his head up. His eyes were red. His whole face was the color of raw liver. "And why not?" he protested. "I am a civilized man. I set things in civilized order. Any civilized person would have done the same."

Corning threw the folder to the floor and paced back and forth across the room.

"*Mijnheer* Masterhoff," Casey said softly, "I am sorry you have been subjected to this. In a way I feel responsible. Mr. Ford was my husband."

"He told me his name was Forster," Masterhoff protested.

"In any event," Casey continued, "whatever he left was intended for me." She held the letter out again for him to see.

"What does it matter now?" Masterhoff gave a heart-rending sigh.

"Because perhaps you can tell me what it was that my husband left for me."

"It's senseless."

"Do you know what it was?" Casey quietly persisted.

Corning stopped his angry pacing and listened.

"You must understand, Mrs. Ford," Masterhoff said defensively. "The envelope was sealed. I would never have opened it. I would never have so violated a client's confidence."

"That's so much shit," Corning spat. Casey threw him a withering look.

"I understand. But it's most important that we know. If you have any idea . . . we won't consider it a breach of trust."

*** **132**

Corning whirled and looked as if he might attack Masterhoff. Casey caught his eye and stopped him again. Masterhoff was aware of none of this interplay. His eyes were down, his forehead cupped in his palm.

"So," Casey patiently continued, "if you do know what was in that envelope I would be grateful if you told me, and I would consider your knowledge a service to your client."

"I know," Masterhoff responded in a voice that barely found its way up from his throat. "I know. But only because I saw him, the man in the ski mask, tear open the envelope when he took it from the file."

Corning stopped pacing, stood rigidly halfway across the room, unwilling to cause Masterhoff's words to be lost by the sound of a footfall, by the sound of a breath.

"What was it?" Casey prodded.

"Such a small thing," Masterhoff groaned. "Such a small thing to make such a fuss about."

"What was this small thing?"

Masterhoff sighed, unstuck his forehead from his palm, and balefully looked at Casey. "It looked to me like a ticket, Mrs. Ford."

"A ticket to what?" She kept darting looks at Corning to keep him away.

"I don't know, Mrs. Ford. I caught only a glimpse when he took it from the envelope. He looked at it. Then he put it back into the envelope and put the envelope into his pocket. But I'm quite sure it was not a ticket to an event like a theater or an opera. It looked like a hat check or perhaps for luggage."

"Do you have any idea which of those it might have been?" Casey asked.

Masterhoff shook his head, his chin down in his chest again. "I don't know, Mrs. Ford. I regret this sincerely."

133 ***

"Do you know if the ticket was from somewhere in Amsterdam?"

Masterhoff didn't even shake his head this time. He just stared down at his ample belly. "I don't know, Mrs. Ford."

He was an utterly defeated man.

He barely protested when Corning dropped the length of clothesline across his chest. He merely looked at Casey with the baleful eyes of a house pet who had been betrayed by his master. Casey stood up and angrily ordered Corning to stop.

Tears began to well up in Masterhoff's eyes, but he made no attempt to struggle.

"We need time," Corning muttered, as he went to work tying a knot. "This won't hurt him."

"The man is terrified."

"He'll call the police as soon as we walk out of here."

"We've nothing to fear from the police."

"We'll be held up with questioning."

"*I'll* call the police if you tie this man down. There is a limit to how far I'll go to help you settle your grievances."

Corning ignored her and threw another loop of cord across Masterhoff's chest and pulled it tight.

"If *you* won't call the police, *I* won't call the police." It was Masterhoff's pleading in a voice as weak and without timbre as a breath of air. Corning was preparing a fresh gag for Masterhoff's mouth. Casey tore the gag out of Corning's hand.

"I warn you, Mr. Corning!"

"*I* have no reason to call the police," Masterhoff continued plaintively. "It was *your* property that was stolen. If you don't mind, I don't mind. I don't want the police looking into my affairs any more than, it appears, you do."

"There's your poor, honest businessman," Corning spat.

"Untie him!" Casey ordered.

"I don't trust him."

"If you don't untie him, you might as well tie me down too, because I won't leave this room until he's free."

Corning hesitated. His eyes blazed. "You don't fully appreciate what is at stake here."

"I do. You made it very clear. But I won't stand by and see an innocent person made to suffer for it. Either you untie him or you go on without me."

Corning's eyes narrowed. He drew in a deep breath. He appeared to expand and grow in height, an even more formidable hulk of a man than he had been before. His hand dipped into his coat pocket and emerged again, almost instantly, the knife blade flashing open as it came. Casey stiffened. Masterhoff sighed with a sound like a punctured tire going flat. Corning slipped the knife blade between Masterhoff's shoulder blades and, with a quick upward movement, sliced through the rope.

"I hope you're a good judge of character, Mrs. Ford," Corning said throatily. He smiled, his customary courtly and considerate expression replacing the fanatic look that had briefly transformed his features.

He carefully closed the knife and dropped it back into his pocket and then turned to Masterhoff. "Remember your promise, old man," he warned. Masterhoff nodded. His head kept on nodding, as if it were attached to a spring and, once having been set in motion, wouldn't stop. "Because," Corning continued, "if the police are brought into this, I *will* come back and cut your ears off." For Casey's benefit he said it lightly, almost jokingly. But Masterhoff got the message.

Casey was profoundly disturbed by Corning's behavior. For a moment she considered dropping the whole business and returning to London. But she couldn't. She was a prisoner, now more than ever, of Ford's legacy. She was constitutionally incapable of allowing the questions raised by the manuscript to go unanswered. Like it or not, their alliance was sealed. Corning needed her brain. And, she reluctantly conceded, the day might come, as they drew closer to their objective, when she would be thankful for Corning's muscle.

As Casey and Corning left the office there was a sharp sound of metal tapping on glass. Casey turned and, in the moment before Corning drew the door shut, saw Masterhoff replenishing his tumbler with gin from the carafe.

25 ***

THEY HURRIED DOWN THE STAIRS and walked quickly away from the house, Corning scanning the street for a cab. A light snow had begun to fall, the eddying wind blowing the powdery flakes like dust swirls around their feet. "The weasel," Corning muttered. "He sold it to them, he must have."

"You overestimate him. He's just a frightened little man."

"Is he? I wouldn't be surprised to see a police car come screaming around the next corner."

"Nonsense. He doesn't want trouble. He's terrified of trouble. He'll sit there and drink enough gin to give him the courage to go home to lunch and face his wife."

"I don't see how Ford could have stored all that gold on one baggage check," Corning said, perplexed. "Do you know how much gold there was? Do you know how much that gold weighs?"

"Unless he transformed it," Casey said.

Corning threw her a startled look. "What do you mean?"

"Traded it in for something else."

Corning's look of surprise changed to one of alarm. "Why would you think that?"

"The manuscript. It indicates that's exactly what he did."

A cab came swinging around the corner. Corning shouted and held up his hand. The cab stopped and backed up to them.

"We've got to get out of Amsterdam," Corning said to Casey. "The first train out. Then we'll think. I don't trust that weasel back there not to turn us in." Corning opened the door for Casey and got in after her.

The cab sped through the snowy streets, taking them back over the same route they had traveled less than thirty minutes before. Casey tapped Corning on the arm to get his attention. "See if you can get us a train south, through Switzerland. I've got a pretty damn sure certain feeling that whatever was on that baggage check, it's going to take our man in the ski mask to Lugano."

"Why Lugano?" Corning asked skeptically.

Casey tapped the manila envelope. "Because there's a page in here describing a transfer of properties in a bank vault. The name of the bank isn't mentioned, nor is the city. Maybe the baggage ticket they took from Masterhoff has that specific information. But Charles sent me his first draft of that page in a letter months ago as a sample of things to come. He never sent me any more pages . . . until I was handed the manuscript in Salisbury. But that page I remember. And I remember the postmark on the envelope it came in. It was Lugano."

The cab turned into the Damrak, with the massive wall of the railroad station rising at the far end.

"And if we miss them in Lugano?"

"Then there's one more chance to intercept them."

"Where is that?"

"Back here. Whatever is in Lugano must be brought back here to be converted again."

"You're certain of this?"

"If Masterhoff proved true. And if Lugano turns out to be true . . . yes. This would be the end of the line."

Corning mulled this over for a while, then whispered

exultantly, "Diamonds! He must have traded the gold for uncut diamonds."

"Possibly."

"It must be. This is the diamond finishing capital of the world." He looked at her accusingly. "I should have tied that old man down. You knew we would have to come back to Amsterdam."

"What good would it have done to tie him down? He'd surely have been released before we returned. If someone had found him tied down the police certainly would have been brought in, whether he wanted it or not."

"Yes," said Corning, "Perhaps you're right."

He remained silent, brooding, thoughtful, until the cab drew up at the entrance to the station. He and Casey got out of the cab and stood shivering while Corning fished in his pockets for money to pay the driver.

"I'll buy the train tickets. You go directly to the platform," he said. "The less we're seen together, the better. When you see me get on the train, you follow. I'll pass your ticket to you as soon as we're under way. Then we'll separate again until we arrive." Casey nodded and hurried into the station. Corning paid the cabby, watched him drive away, and then flagged down the next cab in the line. He gave the driver Masterhoff's address.

26 ***

I CAN'T STAND HERE FOREVER, Wernicke thought as he studied himself in the mirror over the sink in the men's washroom on the platform level of Central Station and carefully parted, combed and reparted his hair. He had been working at his hair for three or four minutes now, a pretext for remaining in the men's room. But the man using the urinal nearby had been there for an unconscionably long time, too. Either he had just come in from a very long journey, or he was a timid queer waiting for some sign from Wernicke before hazarding an overture. Perhaps the man wasn't taking that long, Wernicke thought. Perhaps I'm just edgy.

In the locked stall behind him, Wernicke could hear the sound of papers being unfolded and opened. It sounded as if someone were reading a newspaper in there. Wernicke knew it was Rawlings, carefully going through the contents of the briefcase they had picked up ten minutes before in the Left Luggage department. They had gone to a bench in the waiting room and opened the case, and found it stuffed with what appeared to be several Swiss newspapers. Despairingly they had snapped the case shut again and gone to find someplace private where the contents could be carefully broken down and sifted through without attracting attention. Surely Ford hadn't taken the trouble to store a briefcase stuffed with nothing but old newspapers.

Wernicke glanced to the side and caught the queer

watching him. Perhaps he wasn't a queer. Perhaps he was a cop who thought Wernicke was a queer. Perhaps he was a metropolitan cop. Perhaps Masterhoff had somehow untied his ropes, or been untied by someone else, and had turned in an alarm. Still, there would be no reason in the world for a policeman to suspect him. There was no means of identification. He had worn a ski mask.

The man at the urinal zipped up his fly at last, approached Wernicke, and said something in Dutch. Wernicke shook his head no to whatever it was the man was saying and decided he'd better leave.

"Do you speak English?" the man asked as Wernicke turned. "French?" Wernicke kept walking. "I only wanted to know if you could tell me the time."

Wernicke let the door slam shut behind him, walked down the platform a way, and turned around again. The man hadn't followed him; hadn't, in fact, come out of the washroom. Wernicke sat down on a bench and waited. Still the man didn't come out.

Two men just off a train went into the washroom, stayed a few minutes, and left. Wernicke was beginning to become concerned about Rawlings. Another minute and he would have to risk going back inside to see what was happening.

The washroom door opened and Eric came out carrying the briefcase. He looked puzzled for a moment as he scanned the platform. Wernicke got up from the bench. Eric caught sight of him and moved quickly toward him, swinging his lame leg like a counterweight.

Wernicke kept his eye on the washroom door to see if Eric would be followed by the man who had been at the urinal. The man didn't come out.

Eric nodded to Wernicke and Wernicke fell into step beside him. "We've got a little problem."

"The chap in the restroom?" Warnicke asked.

"I wish that was all. He was just a queer."

"He was the reason I left. I wasn't sure what he was."

"I know. I heard him ask you the time. He asked everyone the time. He asked me the time when I came out of the stall, and all the while he had a fancy gold wristwatch on his arm. Just a queer."

"Was the briefcase empty?"

"No. I found a key taped inside one of the newspapers. A key to a bank vault. Bank of Lugano."

"Then we have it. What's the problem?"

"To use the key we need a signature, and I don't even have a sample."

"Ford's signature?"

"I've got a sample of that. I don't think that's the one we need." They started down the double flight of stairs to the waiting room, Rawlings holding onto the railing for support.

"Whose signature, then?" Rawlings looked grim. Wernicke grabbed Rawlings' arm. "His wife's?"

"That's a very good guess."

"Do you suppose they were together in this all along?"

"I'm beginning to wonder," Rawlings said.

"I wonder about something else," Wernicke said. "What if Ives had a sample of her signature and is already in Lugano?"

"If he is, he's stalled. We have the key."

"Do we? If he's one step ahead of us, why doesn't *he* have the key? What if he planted that baggage ticket at Masterhoff's? What if we're being led nowhere?"

As they rounded the turn in the landing Rawlings stopped short so abruptly that he tottered for a moment. Wernicke turned. "What's wrong?"

"Keep walking," Rawlings whispered urgently. "I'll meet

you in the restaurant downstairs." Wernicke followed Rawlings' eyes down to the bottom of the stairway.

"What's she doing here?"

"Keep walking. She doesn't know you. I don't want her to see you with me."

Casey Ford was just starting up the stairs to the train platform.

Halfway to the first landing Casey glanced up, her eyes going wide with astonishment as she saw Eric standing there, looking debonair and businesslike, a handsome leather briefcase in hand. A look of delighted surprise crossed his face as he caught sight of her. He waved his free hand and limped down to meet her.

"Casey!" he cried. "What on earth are you doing here?"

She looked flustered for a moment and then recovered. "Business," she said breezily. "There was a message waiting for me when I left you last night. I had to fly down here first thing this morning. And you?" Casey asked.

"Business, too. I just arrived. What a small world. What a pity we didn't know. We might have traveled together."

Casey shrugged. "Ships in the night."

She glanced down at the briefcase in Rawlings' hand and her heart jumped.

"Will you be returning to London?" Rawlings asked.

"I'm on my way now."

"I'd like us to get together again."

"Wonderful."

"Same hotel?"

"Same hotel. Well . . ." She had trouble keeping her eyes off the briefcase.

"Well . . . I suppose you have a train to catch?"

"Right," she answered, relieved. She waggled her fingers at him and started up the stairs again. She didn't dare look

143 ***

back, not yet. She wondered if Eric was aware that she was lying, as she most certainly was aware that he was. She had seen Charles Ford's monogram on the briefcase.

At the landing she stopped and hazarded a glance over the rail in time to see Rawlings disappear into the restaurant on the main floor. She continued up to the platform, walked as quickly as she could to the far stairway, restraining her impulse to break into a run. She hurried down the back stairway to the main floor and followed the arrows in the passageway to the ticket booths. There were two or three people in line. But no Corning. Breathlessly she retraced her steps, returning up the back stairway and across the length of the platform, wondering where Corning was, wondering if he might not have been coming up the main stairs as she was going down the back. But Corning was nowhere to be seen on the platform.

She returned to the landing and remained standing there, hoping there was no back way out of the restaurant, hoping Corning would hurry wherever he was. She knew that if Eric left the restaurant, she couldn't follow him. He knew her too well. And then she realized that whether or not she followed him didn't matter. For both of them the next stop was Lugano. Eric would be there sooner or later. And if he got there sooner, he couldn't make a move without her. She knew it. She wondered if he knew it, too. She was angry and embittered. All his current courting of her had been hollow, as it had been years ago. He had used her now, as he had used her then, to help unlock Charles' secret. And she felt like a fool for having allowed herself to be taken in by him both times. Yet she wondered, knowing all she knew about him now, why she still felt so strongly drawn to him. The bastard was a charmer . . . just as Ford had been . . . just as her father had been. Perhaps her fascination for charming bastards could be traced back to her old man.

Where the hell was Corning? For all his grossness and violent lapses, he must be an O.K. guy. She felt no affection for him at all.

27

CORNING SAT HUNCHED FORWARD, squinting across the driver's shoulders through the pie-wedge space that had been brushed clean on the windshield by the wipers. He surveyed the street warily as the cab approached Masterhoff's building. The snow was falling more heavily in big white flakes, and visibility was poor. But there seemed to be no unusual activity in the street; in fact there was almost a total absence of life and movement. The snow had driven people indoors. It appeared that Masterhoff had so far kept his word. There were no police cars in evidence.

He looked at his watch. It had taken him five minutes in the cab from the station to this point. Not bad. Ten more minutes and he should be back in the station. A long ticket line and inquiries about timetables could account for the delay if Casey Ford should question him.

He got out of the cab at the end of the block before his destination and started toward the nearest building as the cab drove away. Then he reversed his direction and walked quickly toward Masterhoff's place.

He had already decided how he would do it, with the knife across Masterhoff's throat. One deep cut from ear to ear and it would be all over. He would have to remember to make a few tentative nicks immediately afterward, to make it look authentic, as if the old man had tested the feel of the blade against his flesh before getting up the courage to make the fatal move. Of course there would be no note. He couldn't manage to counterfeit that. But Masterhoff gave every indication of being an alcoholic. Just an old rummy succumbing to a suicidal fit of depression. The medical examiner's files must be bulging with similar cases.

As he started up the outside steps to Masterhoff's building, Corning wished there were some other way. He regretted having to leave an excellent knife behind clenched in the old man's fist, a weapon that might be traced. Still, if Casey Ford was correct, if they did have to return to Amsterdam, the chance of the knife being traced was less formidable than the risk involved if Masterhoff remained alive and talked to the police. As for the knife . . . he could get another. They made excellent knives in Switzerland.

Corning opened the outer door and hesitated. Behind the frosted glass of the inside door he could see the silhouette of a figure coming down the stairs. Corning cursed under his breath as he pulled shut the outer door and took the stone steps two at a time down to the street. He slipped on the snow at the bottom and sustained a ringing crack on the wrist as he reached out for the support of the iron balustrade. He hurried away from the building, clutching his painful right foream with his left hand. He knew it wasn't broken but it hurt like hell. Chalk up another grievance against the old man.

Thirty rapid paces away from the building he slowed, turned, and started casually back, his head tucked down in his collar, in case the man coming out of the building should be coming his way.

The man wasn't. He was walking gingerly across the road, toward the bridge that spanned the canal on the other side of the Herengracht. It was Masterhoff; the rotund profile, bald head and fringe of white hair were unmistakable

147 ***

even through the snowfall. He drew slowly away, a dimly seen figure in a grainy photograph.

Corning glanced up and down the street. There was no one else in sight and the visibility was poor. He could barely see the other side of the canal. Walking quickly he could catch Masterhoff somewhere in the middle of the bridge. A quick, hard shove and the old man would go toppling over the guard rail down through the thin ice cover on the canal. If he was found before spring the alcohol in his stomach would testify to the accidental nature of his passing. A man, unsteady on his feet, leaning over, perhaps to vomit, leaning over too far. Much cleaner, far less risky than a knife job. God must be on my side, Corning thought cheerfully as he began to follow the old man.

Corning stayed on his side of the Herengracht, walking directly back toward Masterhoff's building until the old man started across the bridge. Then Corning crossed the street, moving quickly along behind the old man, rapidly closing the distance between them.

Masterhoff was just starting down the far side of the bridge, and Corning was no more than ten paces behind him, his footsteps muffled by the thickening carpet of snow. Five more seconds and it would be all over. The old man looked so pitifully cold and uncomfortable that Corning believed he would be doing him a service putting him out of his misery.

Suddenly the old man stopped. A car had come cruising onto the bridge, headlights glowing dimly against the white-out of the snowfall. Corning turned away to face the canal, watching out of the corner of his eye as the vehicle slowly approached. A taxicab.

Masterhoff raised his hand. Corning watched in dismay as the cab stopped, watched the old man walk spraddle-legged out into the road, open the door, and get in.

*** **148**

Corning cursed under his breath and kept his head averted as the cab started up and slowly continued across the bridge. He watched it make a careful U-turn on the other side, almost directly in front of Masterhoff's building. He averted his head again as the cab came back across the bridge in the direction Masterhoff had originally been walking. He heard the whisper of the tires on the new snow as the cab passed him. He faced around again and watched as it vanished into the swirling snowfall on the other side. As it turned off the bridge, its right rear signal light appeared to be winking mockingly.

Stopped cold, a thought came that had eluded him in his impulsive rush to erase the old man. There was no need to return to Amsterdam at all. Perhaps Ford had arranged to sell the diamonds here. But Holland wasn't the only country in the world with a market for uncut stones.

Corning checked his wristwatch. Only eleven minutes had elapsed since he'd left Casey.

28 ***

MASTERHOFF GOT OUT OF THE CAB, trudged across the pavement and up the three stone steps to the door of his house. He stomped his feet to knock the snow off his shoes and reached into his pocket for the key. Then he changed his mind. He let the key fall back into his pocket and pressed the bell. He was home earlier than was his custom and he didn't want to startle his wife.

Ordinarily a jolly and gregarious woman, Frieda had lately become a victim of vague insecurities and sudden and surprising fits of crying. Perhaps she was entering the change of life. Perhaps the dank prison of winter had begun to erode her spirit as it had Masterhoff's. He stomped his feet again while he waited for her to answer, and tucked his hands into his pockets and his chin down into his collar to keep warm.

The lock clicked, the door opened a crack, then swung wide. Frieda Masterhoff was as round and red-cheeked as her husband and approximately the same age, though her hair, wound in a bun at the top, was still golden.

"You're early," she said with concern. "Is something wrong?"

"Everything's quite all right," said Masterhoff, stepping in and unbuttoning his overcoat. *Mevrouw* Masterhoff helped him off with the coat, shook it out, and hung it on a wooden peg near the door while her husband leaned against the wall for support, raised a foot, and, grunting, pulled off his shoe. "There was just a little trouble with the telephone and I have some calls to make." He removed his other shoe and set it beside the first one under his coat.

"Will you be returning to the office?"

"Of course."

"I'll have your lunch in a few minutes."

"No hurry. I have those calls to make." He patted her ample hip and, in his stockinged feet, lumbered up the narrow stairway to his study. As Frieda Masterhoff watched her husband climb the stairs her thoughts were ambivalent, loving and troubled. Her man, she knew, must have something on his mind. He had been behaving strangely lately, edgy and withdrawn despite the outward gestures of affection, like the pat on the hip, which were given absently and more by rote than with feeling. He was drinking, too. She wondered if he had found another woman. She herself, she knew, was not all that she once had been. But that was impossible, irrational suspicion. Where would they meet? He was home at lunchtime every day and never spent an evening without her. Perhaps he was going through a change of life as she was. She heard the door to the study shut. She sighed, shook her head as if that would clear it, and hurried to the kitchen in the back.

On the second floor, Masterhoff closed the study door, padded to the window behind his desk, and took the telephone directory off the wide sill. He found the number for maintenance and repairs, sat down behind his desk, and dialed. He gave his name, office address, and telephone number to the clerk at the other end of the line and requested a service man, explaining that carpet cleaners had been at work in his office and had accidentally broken his phone cable loose from the wall. Then he hung up, lit a small cigar, sat for a moment drumming his fingers on the desk and composing his thoughts.

151 ***

He rose, padded to a shelf displaying an assortment of liquor bottles and tumblers, poured a thimbleful of gin into a glass and returned with it to his desk. He took a sip of the gin and then lifted the receiver and dialed another number, this one from memory. He heard the phone ring once and then hung up, waited thirty seconds, and dialed again. He swung around in his chair and watched the snow falling with increasing density outside his window and mentally counted as the phone rang once, twice, three times. He hung up, waited fifteen seconds more and dialed again. This time the phone at the other end was picked up on the first ring.

"I had a visitor today," Masterhoff said quietly. There was a pause while he listened to an inquiry from the other end. "*Both* parties," Masterhoff replied. "If they had arrived any closer together they would have passed each other in the corridor." A pause. "Frankly, I wish I had never become involved." Then he became agitated. "No, of course I don't choose to return my fee. I couldn't if I wanted to. But I will tell you this much. I hadn't bargained for anything like the fellow who came in with Mrs. Ford. I think if she hadn't been present he wouldn't have been averse to butchering me on the spot. As it was, he returned and followed me when I left the office. . .

"A big man with a pitted face. A very nasty character. As it was I had to play the pathetic old jellyfish to get by . . . whimpering and all . . . but I don't think that would have moved him in the least if Mrs. Ford hadn't been there. By the way, if you should try to reach me at the office, you may find the phone out of order for a day or two. The wire was cut. I'm lucky it was not my throat."

Masterhoff hung up the phone, finished his gin, and padded out of the study and down the stairs to lunch.

*** 152

29

RAWLINGS SLAMMED DOWN THE PHONE and turned, an expression of such disgust on his face that Wernicke knew that something must be wrong.

Wernicke was sitting at a small table in a corner of the crowded restaurant near the steamed-over windows. The atmosphere was stultifying, heavy with the smells of bodies, food, and damp wool. Ford's empty briefcase was resting on the floor against his leg. He dipped his spoon mechanically in and out of the cup of cocoa on the table in front of him, trying to cool it, but his eyes were on Rawlings as he threaded his way among the tables back across the restaurant toward Wernicke.

"Trouble?" Wernicke asked rhetorically.

"The damned airlines. Their schedules are a mess. There's a blizzard moving in across the North Sea. I finally got a flight . . . to Milan. Three o'clock. I'll have to make my way back to Lugano from there."

"And me?" Wernicke asked.

"I want you to follow Mrs. Ford."

"Then we separate? Is that wise? If Ives hasn't sent us off on a wild goose chase, if he's actually in Lugano, he may be waiting for you."

"For the time being we have no alternative. I don't know in whose name that box in Lugano is registered. If it's in Ford's name, I have samples of his signature; I can manage. If it's in Casey's name I must know where we can reach her on short notice. She told me she was going back to London. But I doubt it."

"How will you find me if you need me?" Wernicke asked.

"You'll have to contact me. I'll wait for your calls at noon, six in the evening, and midnight."

"Where?"

"I don't know Lugano. I'll buy a Michelin guide to the city. You buy one too. Find the name of the hotel in the second-class category which is last in alphabetical order. That's where I'll be."

"What about train tickets? I don't know where she's booked for."

"You'll have to buy them from the conductor on the train. Buy a ticket to the end of the line, no matter where the train is headed."

"I hope you won't need her signature. Terrorizing women is not quite my line."

Rawlings smiled wanly, recalling Dorff. "Thank God for that. No. You just stay with her. I'm the one who will have to persuade her. But I agree with you, I hope it's not necessary. Now you'd better get up on the platform. I'll pay the check here and get rid of the briefcase."

"Good luck," Wernicke said.

"We'll both need a little of that," Rawlings replied.

It was ten minutes past twelve noon. He signaled the waitress and paid his bill.

ALBERT CORNING GLANCED UP at the station clock as he entered the downstairs waiting room. Just a little over fifteen minutes had elapsed since he'd left Casey Ford. He turned right, down the corridor to the ticket windows, and bought two seats for the one o'clock train bound for Milan via Basel and Lugano. By twelve-twenty he was standing beside Casey on the platform, apologizing for his delay with the excuse that he had to wait in one line for train information and then wait in another line for the tickets.

"I looked for you in the ticket line," Casey said accusingly.

Corning looked flustered. "I had to go out to the bank to change some money. Why didn't you wait here on the platform as I asked you to?"

"Because on my way to the platform I saw the man who picked up Charles' baggage check at Masterhoff's."

Corning's jaw tightened. He had to strain to keep his voice from rising. "Is he here now?"

"He went into the restaurant on the ground floor ten or fifteen minutes ago."

Corning turned and started for the stairs. Casey took hold of his arm, stopping him. "He isn't there anymore. He left the station about five minutes before you came up."

Corning stared at her. "How can you be sure this was the man?"

"Because he was carrying Charles' briefcase."

"How can you be sure?" Corning rasped.

"Because the initials on the case were C. F."

"A lot of men have names beginning with C. F."

"Not this man's. It was Eric Rawlings."

Corning went gray. "Rawlings! Describe him," he demanded hoarsely.

"You told me you knew him."

"I told you we have been stalking each other for a lifetime. But I have never actually laid eyes on him. It's as if he were a phantom." Beads of sweat were beginning to errupt around Corning's mouth. "Describe him to me," he said with increasing urgency.

"Tall. Six feet, at least. But very slim . . . ascetic looking.

155 *****

He walks with a limp. Extremely handsome, extremely fine features. Pale brown hair, almost blond, mixed with gray. He must be in his middle forties." She paused, then continued softly, almost reflectively. "There are deep lines in the face. Up close you can see them. I thought once they were lines of suffering. Now I see them as hard lines, cynical lines. Funny, isn't it, how circumstance can change one's point of view?"

"What was he wearing?" Corning snapped impatiently.

"Oh . . . a swell dresser, our Eric. A gray coat, beautifully tailored, with lambswool collar. He could pass for a statesman . . . a diplomat. A young Anthony Eden, that would describe him."

Corning dabbed at his sweaty mouth with a handkerchief. He thought for a moment, seemed to hesitate, then reached into his pocket and took out the train tickets. He handed them to Casey. "You go on to Lugano. Wait for me there."

"And what will you do?"

"Find him! If he's in Amsterdam I must find him."

"You'll find him in Lugano, not Amsterdam. And you won't even have to look for him. He'll come looking for me."

30 ***

In his room at the Hotel Nikolas in Basel, Wernicke checked his wristwatch. It was eleven-fifty-five P.M. He stubbed out his cigarette in the ashtray he had placed on the windowsill and got up from the chair near the window from which, for the past two hours, he had been keeping watch on the entrance to the Hotel Stutz across the way. He walked to the bed and picked up the Michelin guidebook, opening it to the page he'd marked listing hostelries in Lugano. He tapped the phone cradle for the operator and gave her the number. Then he hung up, lit another cigarette, and stood by the window, waiting for her to ring him back.

Across the street, in his room in the Hotel Stutz, Albert Corning was also working with a guide book open to Lugano. He had been on the phone for nearly an hour, running up a hefty bill, calling hotel after hotel in that city to the south, asking each time to speak to Eric Rawlings. He had gone about his work patiently and methodically. Beginning at the top of the list of first-class hotels and working down, ringing his own operator, giving the number, waiting for the connection to be made, remaining undaunted when the operator at the other end had replied that there was no Eric Rawlings registered. Corning was now well into the second-class hotel listings.

"Hotel Paris," answered the operator at the other end.

"May I speak to Mr. Eric Rawlings?" Corning politely inquired, as he had already done a dozen times this night.

There was a pause while the operator checked her register. And then there was the reply that caused Corning's heart to leap.

"Mr. Rawlings' line is busy at the moment. Will you wait?"

"No, thank you," Corning replied, camouflaging his jubilance with businesslike nonchalance. "I'll call back."

"Is there a message?"

"No, thank you. I'll call back."

"DID I WAKE YOU, ERIC?" Wernicke asked. He had just gotten through to Rawlings.

"Certainly not. I've been waiting. Where are you calling from?"

"Basel. It looks like they're heading for Lugano, too."

"They?"

"Yes . . . *they!* But of course you couldn't know. She is traveling with a companion."

"You make it sound ominous."

"It is ominous. Her traveling companion is Kornhardt."

There was a pause at the other end of the line and then Rawlings' voice again, edged with alarm. "Are you sure?"

"I have only his description to go by, just as you do. He's a little older and a little heavier than the last time he was spotted. And of course I couldn't get close enough to see if he had that phony tattoo on his wrist. But it's Kornhardt."

"Then she's his hostage."

"No. She's free as a bird and apparently traveling with him because she has chosen to do so."

"I can't believe that."

"You had better, Eric. She is traveling under no duress whatsoever."

"You couldn't get close to them. How do you know he isn't holding a gun on her . . . or a knife? He's supposed to be very handy with a knife."

"I didn't have to be breathing down their necks to observe them during the trip to Basel. In Basel we missed our connection to Lugano because of delays due to the storm. I followed him to the information window. I suppose he was inquiring about the next train out, which is tomorrow morning. All this while, she stood twenty yards off, in a crowded waiting room, with the usual complement of station guards and police about. If she had wanted help, or to escape, she had every opportunity."

"Then she can't know who Kornhardt is."

"I hope you're right, Eric."

"Stay with them until Lugano. Find out where they stop. Then contact me. I must speak to her. If she has been misled by Kornhardt . . ."

"What if she hasn't been misled? What if she knows exactly what she's doing?"

"She can't know. He'll never let her live after he's finished with her."

"Is she that important to you?"

There was a pause. "She's important to all of us. The vault is in her name."

31

THE MORNING TRAIN FROM BASEL threaded its way like a dark worm through the snowy mountain passes and then burrowed into the St. Gotthard tunnel. It came out at the end into a scene of startling color after the glacial fastnesses of the north.

"My God!" Casey exclaimed as the train slowed and jerked and hissed its way into a Lugano suburb aptly named Paradiso. "It's like the Riviera."

A rainbow of pastel-tinted stucco houses climbed the sloping hillsides in a gentle arc around the shoreline of a deep blue lake. Incredibly, there were palm trees . . . palm trees in Switzerland, and laurel, and blossoming forsythia. She opened the window in their compartment, squinting against the brightness of the sunshine, and found the air warm and humid, balmily tropical.

"I can't believe we're still in Switzerland," Casey said. She unfolded a tourist brochure she'd picked up in Basel and read: *Lugano, shielded by mountains from the chill winds of the north, warmed by the waters of its splendid lake, soothing to the nervous system, health-giving to the heart, sedative to the bloodstream and mucous membrane.* . . . She laughed. "They make it sound like something that should be licensed by the FDA."

"FDA?" Corning asked sullenly.

"Food and Drug Administration. An American institution." Casey took a deep breath of the balmy air. "But you know, they're right. It *is* good for the mucous membrane. It certainly beats hell out of steam heat. I must remember to come here some day."

"I can see why Ford did."

"Yes. He always liked easy living. Poor Charles."

"Easy living wasn't the only thing a man like Ford would find attractive about this place. Italy is just across the lake. This place is a smuggler's paradise."

WERNICKE FOLLOWED THEIR CAB to the Hotel California and watched them go in. Then he looked around for a place from which he might keep the hotel under surveillance while he made his phone call to Rawlings. There was a cafe with an outdoor terrace at the end of the block diagonally across from the California. He crossed the street and walked quickly to the cafe. He should have waited a minute longer.

Corning let Casey book their rooms and left the hotel almost immediately after bringing her into the lobby. By the time Wernicke had reached the cafe, Corning was in a taxi on his way to the Hotel Paris. While Wernicke resumed his vigil at an outside table and asked the waiter if he might use the phone, Corning was approaching the entrance to Rawlings' hotel.

Had the phone in the cafe not already been in use by another customer, Rawlings might at least have been warned that Corning was in town. He might have been on his guard when the knock came at his door and the man outside announced himself as the "porter."

Rawlings opened the door. His benignly inquisitive expression gave way to gaping astonishment. In a single in-

161 ***

stant he recognized his visitor as Kornhardt and felt the breathtaking punch of the knife ramming in under his ribs. He was already beginning to sag as Corning butted him backward into the room. He collapsed against the foot of the bed, his torso folded over on his legs like an unstrung marionette.

Corning left the knife in him lest, pulling it out, he uncork a gusher and stain his clothes. He took quick and efficient inventory of the room and found no sign of Ford's briefcase. Rawlings must have dumped it somewhere along the way. The room key lay on the dresser and, surprisingly to Corning, a photocopy of Charles Ford's manuscript. The closets and the drawers held nothing of interest.

Corning peeled off his gloves and knelt beside Rawlings' body and gingerly began going through his pockets. He was startled by the harsh ring of the phone on the night table. He stood up and watched the phone, as if it were a live presence in the room. It continued to ring insistently in short, abrasive burps. He drew on his left-hand glove, picked up the phone, and grunted into the mouthpiece as if just wakened from sleep.

"Eric?" the voice at the other end inquired. Corning grunted again. "This is Wernicke," the voice hurried on. "Mrs. Ford and Kornhardt just checked into the Hotel California." Corning's stomach tightened. They had been under surveillance for God knew how long and he had been totally unaware. Even worse, he had been identified. He could only hope that Rawlings and the man on the phone were the only ones this close to him.

"I'm in a cafe down the street from their hotel," Wernicke reported. "Shall I stay here or come up?"

Corning's panic began to subside, displaced by clear, icy calm. He ran his tongue over his lips. Corning knew how he would dispose of this faceless pursuer.

"Are you there, Eric?" Wernicke asked. In reply, Corning groaned as if in pain.

"Are you all right, Eric?" Wernicke asked, his voice rising with alarm.

Corning kept silent.

"I'm coming, Eric," Wernicke assured him. "Hang on."

Corning groaned once more for good measure as the connection was broken. He looked at his watch. He would have at least five minutes' leeway. It had taken him that long to get from the California to the Hotel Paris by cab. He crossed quickly back to the body and resumed his search of the pockets. He found what he was looking for in Rawlings' passport case, a flat brown envelope containing a small bank vault key.

He tucked the key into his own pocket, drew on his gloves again, wiped the passport case clean of fingerprints, and dropped it onto the night table.

He looked at his wristwatch and calculated that he had two minutes to spare before turning in the alarm. He flashed the operator and gave the number of the Hotel California and asked to be connected to Casey's room.

"Meet me at the bank of Lugano in fifteen minutes. If I'm not there when you arrive, wait for me inside. I have the key."

"How . . . ?"

"I picked his pocket," Corning said, smiling to himself. "He'll never know."

"You're very versatile," Casey congratulated him.

"Fifteen minutes, Bank of Lugano," he repeated, his eye on the sweep second hand of his wristwatch. Then he hung up. He let twenty seconds more elapse and figured that Wernicke should be entering the hotel just about now. He flashed the operator, tapping the cradle repeatedly, simulating a matter of great urgency. When the operator finally picked up he cried out without preamble, "This is Rawlings in 205. Police! Hurry! Help!" Then he knocked the phone from the table, picked up the copy of the manuscript, and left the room, making certain that the door didn't snap locked behind him.

He took the stairs down at a leisurely pace, stopped for a moment on the landing just above the lobby, and watched, amused, as a man hurried to the elevator. He hoped it was Wernicke.

He resumed his descent on the stairway, crossed the lobby, and passed out into the street. He could hear the whooping claxons of the police cars in the distance. He crossed to the side of the street opposite the hotel and watched as the police cars came careening around the corner and squeaked to a halt. There was a hectic thudding and thumping of steel doors as the policemen rushed from their cars into the hotel. Soon Corning was just another figure in a gathering crowd of curious onlookers. Mentally he tried to calculate how wealthy he would be in just a little while. He would have to stop on his way to the bank and buy a suitcase to pack the diamonds into. He would also have to begin considering the problem of disposing of Mrs. Ford after he had the stones safely in hand. There was the sound of another claxon as an ambulance rounded the corner and lurched to a stop alongside the police cars.

Corning remained standing in the crowd. He decided that perhaps he'd better purchase a new knife on his way to the bank as well as a suitcase. He watched with satisfaction as two of the policemen emerged from the hotel hustling a protesting Wernicke between them into one of the cars. Farewell, Mr. Wernicke, thought Corning as he began to ease his way back out of the crowd when a sudden gasp from the onlookers caused him to turn again in the direction of the hotel. The ambulance attendants were bringing out the stretcher bearing Rawlings' body. From where he stood he could see the irregular crimson stain on the sheet tucked around Rawlings' chest. But there was something wrong with the picture. The sheet wasn't drawn up over Rawlings' head. And a policeman, walking beside the stretcher, was carrying a portable oxygen tank with the mask clamped down over Rawlings' face. Corning, to his horror, realized that Rawlings must still be alive.

32

CASEY WAS WAITING in the bank when Corning arrived. He was carrying a new soft-sided tartan suitcase and seemed nervous and agitated.

"Is there some trouble?" Casey asked.

"No. None at all." But the edge in his voice belied his words.

"The vault's downstairs. I've already asked the guard."

"Good," he said as he grimly followed her to the stairway.

"Something *is* wrong."

"Nothing. I just want to clear out of town before Rawlings finds his key missing."

"You were sure he wouldn't."

"Perhaps I was too sure," he said.

They went down a flight of marble stairs to the basement of the bank where they were confronted by a barred gate like the entrance to a cell-block. An attendant sat at a desk inside, profile to them, working methodically on a pile of file cards. Corning took the key out of his pocket and tapped on the bars with it. The attendant looked up. Corning held the key up for him to see. The attendant pressed a button on his desk, a buzzer sounded, releasing the lock on the gate. Corning pushed and the gate swung open.

"Let's hope," Corning said under his breath, "that the box is in your name."

"Let's hope he forged it well," Casey murmured.

They approached the attendant, who tore a printed form off a pad and slid it across the desk to them. He took a pencil from a caddy and placed it on top of the form. Casey took a deep breath, let it out slowly, leaned over the desk, and signed her name.

The attendant picked up the paper and looked at it, perplexed. Her signature was a scrawl.

"Ford," Casey said. "Casey R. Ford."

The attendant nodded and crossed to his file cabinet. He pulled out the drawer and walked his fingertips through the cards until he found what he was looking for. He lifted the card half out of the file and glanced back and forth from it to the form Casey had just signed. His eyes moved from the signature to Casey and then to Corning. Casey smiled uneasily. Corning looked grim. The attendant slid the signature check card back into its file and shut the drawer. Then he inclined his head toward Casey. "Your key, please."

Corning handed the key to the attendant. He wished he'd had the presence of mind to give it to Casey before they came down. He was not thinking so coolly and clearly as he should. Rawlings' survival had shaken him. He had taken too much for granted in assuming the knife thrust had been fatal. Surely Rawlings would not pull through. But would he regain consciousness and clear Wernicke before he died? Would Wernicke then lead a whole new team of hounds after him before he could cover his tracks?

The attendant took the key and walked through the eighteen-inch-thick portal of the vault proper. Corning and Casey followed, watched him open a safe door and remove a large metal box. The attendant placed the key on top of the box and ceremoniously carried it out and into one of a group of small private rooms. There was a waist-high formica shelf in the room on which he carefully placed the box, and there was just one chair. Casey and Corning stood uneasily on either side of the chair, until the attendant left them, the door closing behind him with a click.

"Wait," Corning whispered to Casey and moved quickly to the door. "I wouldn't trust that old bastard not to have locked us in and called the police." Corning turned the knob carefully and moved the door just enough to make sure it wasn't locked.

"Yes, sir?" inquired the attendant. He was back at his desk going over his cards.

"We'll call you when we're finished," Corning snapped.

"No need to call. There's a buzzer over the table."

Corning closed the door and turned. Casey already had the box open. From where he stood the box looked empty. He took a quick step to Casey's side and stared down.

A small gray plastic bag, eight inches long and six inches in diameter, lay in the bottom of the box. A square of paper pasted to the side of the bag read, *"Chrysanthemum, Estrella Azul."*

"What the hell is that?" Corning hissed.

"It sounds like a flower," Casey said, bemused.

Impetuously Corning reached into the box, grabbed the bag, and began kneading it with his fingers, confirming tactiley what his eyes had already surmised. "They *aren't* diamonds!" For a moment he stood there, at a loss, balancing the bag in his hand. "It can't weigh more than a few pounds," he muttered in disbelief. "It can't even be gold dust." And then, suddenly, hopefully, "It must be dope! Uncut dope."

"If it is," Casey said coolly, "you're out of luck. It goes straight to the police."

Corning reached into his pocket and flicked open his new knife.

*** **168**

"What's that for?"

"To bloody well find out." He carefully made a small slit in the top of the bag. He tapped a small sample of the contents of the bag into his palm. He studied the tiny brown granules, then he looked at Casey, totally bewildered. "What the bloody hell is it?"

Casey shrugged. "They look like seeds."

"They can't be. That's insane. Someone got here first and left this junk for ballast." In disgust he dropped the bag back into the iron box. More of the dark granules spilled out.

"Why would anyone who had been here bother to leave anything behind?" Casey said levelly.

"Then you tell me what it is, since you pretend to know so much." Corning was growing livid.

"I don't know what it is. But I know where we may find out. And I think we should have this little bag with us when we do." She opened her purse, took out a book of matches, tore out the matches, and then tore the matchbook in half. Using the cardboard of the matchbook as a scoop, she meticulously gathered up the spilled granules and tapped them back into the bag. Corning watched, granite-faced.

"Lend me your knife," Casey said.

Corning didn't move. His knuckles were white around the knife handle.

"Lend me your knife! I have to reseal this damned thing or we'll be spilling it all the way from here back to Amsterdam."

Corning hesitated a moment and then handed over the knife. Casey knicked the thread on one of her coat buttons and carefully drew it out. She repeated the process with another button until she had two lengths of thread, which she tied together. She put the buttons into her pocket and

169 ***

then looped the thread around the top corner of the bag just below where Corning had made the opening. She pulled the thread tight and knotted it. "That will have to do for a while."

Corning picked up his knife, snapped it shut, and slipped it back into his pocket.

Casey transferred the contents of her purse into her coat pockets and packed the plastic bag into her purse. "Next stop, Amsterdam," she said, "the Hotel Krasnapolsky."

"And what's supposed to happen there?"

"We'll see. Meanwhile, I recommend we buy some clothes to go in that suitcase. I'm tired of having bellboys stare at me." She closed the metal safe deposit box, empty now, and rang for the attendant.

33 ***

MASTERHOFF WAS FINDING IT DIFFICULT to concentrate on his ledgers. The blizzard of two days before had ended. But the high winds had not abated. It was another bleak and chilly day in a series of bleak and chilly days, and it depressed him. He poured a measure of gin from his carafe and sipped it, dreaming of spring, dreaming of warmer lands, wondering if, when this sordid business was over, he would have the wherewithal to take himself and Frieda elsewhere when next winter rolled around. Maybe that would be a cure for what ailed them both. He glanced at his watch. In a little while it would be time to trudge home to lunch. Frieda must surely be as weary of the routine as he. He closed his ledger and was about to get up and go to the washroom at the end of the hall when his newly repaired telephone rang. He sighed, lifted the receiver and droned, "Masterhoff."

"Are you alone?" the voice at the other end inquired. Masterhoff's heart leapt. He felt a great weight drop from his shoulders. Perhaps waiting for the call had lain at the root of his malaise rather than the dismal weather.

"Yes," Masterhoff said. "I'm alone."

"Have you seen the Swiss newspapers?" The voice at the other end was edged with excitement.

"Why should I read Swiss newspapers? Things are bad enough here."

"Of course." His caller was most understanding. "Then let me tell you what I read. An item from Lugano. A gentleman attacked in his hotel room by a madman with a knife."

"So?"

"So it's my educated guess that the gentleman who lies critically wounded was the same man who visited you the other day, wearing a ski mask."

"Then the 'madman' must be the one who came in with Mrs. Ford. He was very handy with a knife. Is he still at large?" Masterhoff asked uneasily.

"He was taken into custody at the scene of the crime, in the wounded man's hotel room."

"Thank God for that," Masterhoff said.

"Yes. It's all worked out quite well, quite as I'd hoped it would. They've cancelled each other out."

"Then . . . if our business is finished . . ." Masterhoff tried to approach the matter of his final payment obliquely.

"Not quite finished yet." Masterhoff closed his eyes as if in pain. "Mrs. Ford may be returning to Amsterdam . . . perhaps with a parcel. I will need your help."

"And if she doesn't return to Amsterdam?"

"Then you need trouble yourself no further. I can retrieve the parcel myself in Lugano now that the wolves have eaten each other."

"And my final payment?"

"There can be nothing for either of us until the parcel is in my hands. Now, listen carefully while I tell you what you must do should Mrs. Ford return to Amsterdam. Do you have a pencil and paper handy?"

Masterhoff reached across the desk and picked up a note pad. He began jotting down his instructions with a sinking feeling that he had soiled himself irremediably by entering into this business and that no break from routine or from the dreariness of winter could compensate for the crisis of conscience that confronted him. He wondered if he would find it less difficult to live with himself in the sunshine of Curaçao than in the bleakness of the Amsterdam winters.

34

THE NIGHT CLERK at the Krasnapolsky glanced at the register card and then looked up quizzically. "Miss Ford?" he asked, as if to verify the name she had just entered on the card.

"Yes," Casey replied. "Is something wrong?"

"Not at all. It's just that . . . if you'll wait one moment, I believe we're holding a message for you. Just one moment, please." He turned and went into the small office behind the desk. Through the open door, Casey and Corning could see him shuffling through the papers in a box. In a moment he returned, carrying a small white envelope. "Yes," he said. "Here it is." He looked at the time stamped on the envelope. "It came in just this afternoon."

Casey opened the envelope and took out the note and, with a look of satisfaction, held it out for Corning to see. "Please telephone Masterhoff," it read, "with regard to the disposition of your property." There were two telephone numbers. One for his office. One for his home.

"He's a bit anxious to hear from me, wouldn't you say?" she asked Corning. Then she turned to the clerk. "Do you have a safe for valuables?"

"Certainly. If you have something you wish to deposit now . . ."

"Yes, please." She handed him her purse.

The clerk looked surprised, but he took the purse back

into the office. He attached a tag to it and locked it in the safe. Then he came out and handed Casey her receipt.

They followed the bellboy to the elevator. Upstairs, Corning waited in the hallway while the boy went through the ritual of opening and closing windows and closets in Casey's room. The boy came out, closing Casey's door behind him, and led Corning to his room and repeated the ritual. Corning gave him his tip, waited a few minutes until he was sure the boy had left the hall and then returned down the corridor to Casey's room.

He stopped at her door and was about to knock when, to his astonishment, he heard her talking to someone inside. He hesitated a moment, trying to listen, and then tried the knob. The door opened, revealing Casey seated across the room holding the telephone to her ear with one hand and holding the other hand up in a signal for silence.

Corning closed the door quietly behind him and stood watching as Casey made notes with a pencil on a piece of hotel stationary.

"Yes, *Mijnheer* Masterhoff," she finally said. "I have it all down. Tomorrow at one o'clock." And she placed the receiver gently down in its cradle.

"Well," she said with some satisfaction, "I have just phoned Masterhoff regarding the disposition of the property."

"Did he say what it was?"

"No. It would seem that he is merely acting as middleman for a party who would like to purchase this property from me for a handsome sum of money."

"That bag of . . . junk?" Corning said derisively. "He doesn't know what we found in that vault."

"Maybe not. But I'd like to know what he thought we'd find. And I'd like to know who thought we'd find it. Because that's the man who killed Charles. I'm to bring the package to a luncheon meeting at Masterhoff's home where it can be inspected and where a price can be negotiated with this third party."

"Why in Masterhoff's home? Why not in his office?"

"Maybe he has unpleasant memories of our last meeting in his office," Casey said pointedly.

"Did he mention me?"

"Strangely, no. Although I don't know how he could have forgotten you. He seemed to take it for granted that I was here alone . . . that you had somehow dropped out of the picture. What bothers me is this . . . he gave me detailed instructions for driving there. It seems to be somewhere out on the road to Volendam, about a thirty-minute drive away. Now he's a man who goes home for lunch every day. A half-hour drive each way for lunch every day seems a little much to me."

"That's because you're an American. Europeans do it."

"Well," said Casey, reaching under the night table and coming up with a phone book, "because I'm an American I question it." She began flipping through the pages of the phone book until she found the *M*'s. She ran her finger down the columns of names. She planted her finger under a name halfway down the page and triumphantly held the book up for Corning to see. "There," she said, "Masterhoff, Jan, notary . . . the address in the Herengracht is his office. And, right under it, Masterhoff, Jan . . . . in the Rembrandt-plein. That must be his home. And it's right here in the city. Yes! When I go to that meeting, I want you right behind me."

"I wouldn't dream of having it any other way," Corning assured her.

35 ***

WHEN SHE WOKE THE NEXT MORNING, Casey called down to the desk and made arrangements for a hired car to be delivered at noon. She made a nuisance of herself, insisting that they find an agency that could provide her with an American car, the kind she was accustomed to driving at home. What she really wanted was a *big* car, a wide car, so that Corning could lie down on the floor behind the front seat. She asked for a lap rug, too, to keep the chill off her. She would need it to cover Corning when they arrived at their destination.

Promptly at noon the desk clerk phoned her room and told her that the car was waiting. It was a four-door Chrysler and looked huge and grotesque among the smaller European cars in the street. The man from the rental agency checked her passport and driver's license, showed her how the heat and fan and defroster worked and crowed over the electrically operated windows controlled by a bank of buttons on the driver's armrest. He turned on the radio and lit cigarettes for both of them from the car's glowing lighter. Then he drove around the block twice with her to make sure she could handle the car. He took her deposit and gave her a card with the address to which the car should be returned when she was through with it. She parked the car and went back into the hotel to let Corning know she was ready.

"*Juvrouw*!—ah—Miss Ford—if you please," the desk clerk called to her as she crossed the lobby on her way to the house phone. He held his hand discreetly aloft, a piece of note paper slotted between his fingers.

Casey crossed quickly to the desk, wondering if the note was from Masterhoff, calling for a change in plans.

"The switchboard girl took the call just a moment ago," the clerk explained apologetically as he handed her the note. "Had we known you would be returning so immediately we could have asked the party to hold the line."

She unfolded the paper and dropped her eyes to the name typed in at the bottom of the message. It *wasn't* from Masterhoff. But who, she wondered, was A. Wernicke?

"Eric Rawlings hospitalized," the note read. "He has requested I assist you. Urgent you make no move until my arrival Amsterdam 3 o'clock. Signed A. Wernicke."

No thank you, she thought, as she crumpled the note and stuffed it into her coat pocket. She needed no "assistance" from Eric Rawlings or anyone associated with him. Hospitalized? She'd just bet he was. The whole thing was a cheap ploy to delay her. Well, Eric was out of the running, and good riddance. Bitterly she remembered the tenderness she had once felt for him, and the trust she had placed in him. She picked up the house phone and called Corning to tell him she was ready to go. She glanced up at the clock over the desk. It was twelve-thirty.

IT WAS TWELVE-THIRTY when Masterhoff left his office for his daily walk home to lunch. He trudged across the bridge, his hands thrust deep into his pockets, his coat collar turned up against the biting wind blowing off the canal. He'd had more than his normal ration of gin that morning, but it had

*** **178**

been ineffective in stilling the battle that was raging inside him. He had been debating with himself for hours, trying to persuade himself that no harm would come to the American woman, trying to convince himself that whatever happened, it was the concern of his client and Mrs. Ford. He was just a middleman. He had not embroiled them in this business. They had done that themselves, whatever their motives. He was an honorable man in an honorable profession. He owed this client, as he owed all his clients, his confidence, his silence, the assurance that whatever business they were engaged in, that portion of their business that passed through his hands would be held in the strictest confidence. But he knew, too, that this particular client was like no client he had ever served. He, Masterhoff, was a legitimate businessman, an agent of sorts. But he knew that for the first time in his life he was involved in a business outside the law, and that he might very well be acting as an agent of death. He was being paid entirely too much for his role in this thing for it to be part of any legitimate enterprise. He had allowed himself to be drawn into it out of despair, out of a desperate wish to leave the memory of fifty-odd winters behind him, out of a need to escape. But he was not a criminal. He lacked the constitution for it.

He looked at his watch. It was twelve-thirty-five and, barring a miracle, that woman was on her way to a rendezvous from which she would never return. And he was the Judas who had sent her into the trap. He could not go home and take lunch with his wife and continue through the day as if nothing had happened. He turned and fled back across the bridge to his office, a fat, spraddle-legged old man hounded by invisible furies.

At twelve-forty the Chrysler left the city proper via the Schellingwoude bridge and headed out on the highway that

179 ***

traversed the bleak, flat *poulder;* endless miles of wind-swept land as featureless as the sea from which it had been reclaimed. With spring it would come alive with flowers and farm goods, and cattle would loll about in the sunshine. Now it was a dark and forbidding plain. They drove for ten more minutes across the dead, flat landscape with no more awareness of movement than a passenger feels in an airplane. There were no landmarks to relate to.

"Not very pretty, is it?" Corning muttered. He was sitting up in the back seat with the lap rug folded beside him. "Not even a windmill to look at."

"They bring them out in the spring along with the tulips for the benefit of the tourists."

"How much farther?" Corning asked.

"Ten minutes by the clock. This road is supposed to intersect the IJselmeer Causeway and that's where Master-hoff's house is supposed to be. Unless things change very quickly I don't think we'll find a house there. There's nothing in sight as far as I can see."

"Maybe not. But I think we'll find something."

Five minutes later the road began a gentle arc eastward, heading toward a distant but abrupt rise in the land, like an earthen breastwork running along the rim of the fields.

"That looks like a dike a few miles ahead. Could the crossroad run along the dike?"

Corning unfolded a road map and located their approximate position. "Yes. The road along the dike runs on into Volendam. But Volendam must be five miles down that road. The map shows no residential area anywhere near the crossroads."

"Wait a minute . . ." Casey hit the brake, decelerating the car so suddenly that Corning had to grab the front seat for support.

*** **180**

"Do you see something?"

"No. I just thought of something. Maybe it's not the seeds at all, but the bag itself that's valuable."

"The bag itself is the same kind of plastic they wrap garbage in," Corning grumbled disconsolately.

"But there could be something printed on the inner lining of that bag," Casey said.

"Let's have a look."

Casey steered the car onto the shoulder of the road and set the parking brake.

They carefully poured the seeds out onto the open roadmap on the back seat. They separated the lining from the outer cover of the bag and found nothing. No printing, no map, no instructions. Nothing. Casey held the bag open at the top while Corning funneled the seeds back in. She retied the bag, packed it into the glove compartment, and started the car again.

Five minutes later they were still heading across the featureless *poulder* with the mound of the dike wall growing larger in the near distance. If there was a house of any kind on the near side of the dike they would have sighted it by now. On the far side of the dike there would be nothing but the sea.

A misty rain had begun to fall, drifting sideways at a sharp angle in the high winds raking the flatlands. A gust of wet wind came whooshing through her partially open window, soaking Casey's cheeks. Instinctively she reached for the crank handle and then realized there wasn't one. She found the button on her armrest, pushed it the wrong way, and almost lost control of the car as the window slid down and subjected her to a thorough soaking. She pushed the button the opposite way and the window rolled quickly up, the wind and rain beating angrily against it. She turned on

181 ***

the wipers. For a moment they worked counterproductively, smearing the windshield and cutting her visibility. She slowed until the glass in front of her came clean.

"I see something!" she cried out, peering through the arcing clear area in the windshield.

Corning leaned across her shoulder. "I can't see a thing."

"Up there . . . on the dike, to the left of where our road will meet it."

Corning looked off to the left and saw the dark beetle-shaped object on the dike road. "It looks like a VW."

"And it's not moving. But I'll bet you it's not stopped there because it's run out of gas. When we get onto the dike I'll park across the road from him so that your right hand door is near the slope on the side away from the VW. That way this monster will serve as a shield so you can slip out."

The *poulder* road began to rise to meet the dike as Corning lay down on the floorboards behind the front seat and pulled the blanket over him.

"Can you see anybody yet?" Corning asked.

"No. Just the VW."

"I'd feel a lot easier if I knew whether our friend is in the car or waiting somewhere along the dike."

"He's in the car. The windows are fogged up. I can see which side of the road he's parked on, too. It's the near side. I'll turn left, but watch it when you move out. You'll be leaving the car on the sea side of the dike."

The dike road crossed the *poulder* like the long top bar of the letter T. Casey saw the dead-end warning sign as she came up onto the dike, and she saw the choppy gray water beyond. From the elevation the dike afforded her she could see the huddled rooftops of the village of Volendam a few miles off. She slowed and made her left hand turn and brought the car to a stop on the shoulder of the road across from the Volkswagen. "We're here," she said quietly, without looking around.

"Wait in the car. Let him come to you." Corning's voice came back low and muffled. "Can you see what the slope on the sea side is like?"

Casey slid over in her seat, wiped a clear spot in her misted-over side window, looked down, and slid back behind the wheel. "It looks like earth embedded with rocks. About a forty-five degree slope down."

"I'm getting out now," Corning said.

"Hurry. He's wiping his window clear. I can see his hand." She heard the click as the right rear door opened. There was a rush of chill air. "Be careful," she warned without turning around. "Those rocks will be slippery."

She heard Corning dragging his body along the floor of the car and then the door clicked quietly shut. She hazarded a glance around back. The blanket lay neatly folded on the seat. There was no sign that she had driven out with a passenger.

She shuddered with a chill that had nothing to do with the temperature outside. She felt fearfully vulnerable and alone. Spooky. She cleared away some of the condensation on her side window with the palm of her hand and saw the door of the Volkswagen swing open. She saw a brightly polished black shoe emerge, as if testing the ground, and a neatly pressed trouser leg, banker's gray, and the hemline of a dark woolen overcoat. As the door swung wider, a pair of hunched shoulders appeared as the occupant of the car freed himself from the confines of the front seat. Then the man straightened up as his shoulders and head cleared the door. Casey Ford felt the blood draining from her head, felt herself fading into the fleecy oblivion of a faint.

She clenched her fists and pressed her knuckles into her

183 ***

eyeballs, pressed hard, until it hurt, until starbursts began to go off inside her head, until consciousness prodded by pain began to return. Consciousness, and the thought that she must lock her door against the advance of this specter. But it was too late. Her door was already opening, and the man in the dark woolen overcoat was looking in at her with a peculiarly benign expression.

"Well, don't just sit there with your mouth open," Charles Ford said. "Slide over and let me in. I don't want to die of pneumonia after all I've been through."

Corning lay clinging to the sea side slope of the dike, shielded by the body of the Chrysler. From underneath the chassis he had a view of the feet of the man leaving the Volkswagen and crossing the road. A small man, from the size of his shoes. That was good. He heard the door of the Chrysler open and shut, and the feet vanished. The man was inside. Corning reached into his pocket, drew out his knife, flicked it open and stabbed the white sidewall tire. There was a wheezing sigh, lost in the wind, as the air began to escape. They would never notice the slight, slow settling at the rear. But, should the little man with the bright shoes try to flee in the Chrysler, he wouldn't get very far very fast. Corning thought about spoiling the left rear tire as well, but there was only one spare in the trunk, and he might want to use the Chrysler himself after this meeting was over. He would disable the Volkswagen though, permanently. He tried to stand, slipped, clawed at the roadside and the settling wheel, hung on and regained his footing. But his knife had gone sliding down somewhere among the rocks. He cursed and scrambled up onto the roadside behind the Chrysler. Hunched low, he bolted across the road and threw himself flat on the far side of the Volkswagen.

CASEY SAT NUMBLY on the right-hand side of the front seat, staring at Charles Ford as he made himself comfortable behind the wheel, unbuttoning his overcoat, shaking out his lapels, grinning at her complacently.

"You murdered those two men back in Salisbury," Casey said when she finally found her voice. She sounded bemused, appalled beyond making accusations or passing judgments.

"For Christ's sake, Casey!" Ford looked pained. "What kind of greeting is that?"

"That was the one thing I never believed you capable of."

"I promise you, the world won't miss them. Besides," he asked almost lightly, "would you rather they had murdered me?"

"Would they have?" she asked bitterly.

"Well . . . perhaps not right away," he conceded. "You see, they were supposed to pry certain information out of me first. That gave me a slight advantage. I knew what to expect from them, but they didn't quite know what to expect from me."

"And so you shot them in the back?" She wondered where Corning was and when he would make his move.

Ford sighed, distressed. "Oh, Casey! What a low opinion you have of me. I shot them square in the face." He saw her shudder and spread his hands importuningly. "I had to, if it was to look like what I wanted it to look like. I really carried it off quite well," he added proudly. "But you read about it in the papers."

"Right down to the bit about the advances you made to

185 ***

the delivery boy," she said, making no effort to mask her revulsion.

"Nice bit of plotting, don't you think? Give me your professional opinion."

"I think you're despicable."

Ford shrugged. "I always have been, love. But now I'm also going to be very wealthy, and that will compensate for all the little flaws in my character."

"Not all the money in the world, Charles."

"Oh, Casey!" Ford groaned. "You're so damned self-righteous. You don't know what it is to be deprived."

"Don't I?"

"You mean your difficult childhood?" he said scornfully. "You had nothing to begin with, no promises withheld. You don't know what it means to spend half your life trying to lay claim to what is rightfully yours. And then, when you've got it in your grasp, you discover that all the time someone has been watching you, waiting for you to find it, so they could take it away."

"It didn't belong to you in the first place, Charles."

Ford's face grew hard. The sleepy, bovine eyes narrowed. "You've been talking to the wrong people. Make no mistake about it, the gold belonged to me. *All* of it. The two men who died in Salisbury were in the pay of a pack of scavengers. They expected to enter the cottage and persuade me to give it up to them. An easy job, they thought. I have a reputation for gutlessness. But in this case my weakness was my strength. They never expected that the hare would be waiting for the hounds with a loaded shotgun." Droplets of sweat had begun to form on Ford's forehead despite the cold. "It takes very little strength to kill with a shotgun, Casey. It's not like a knife or a club or a fist. It takes very little skill. It's almost like a toy." His voice grew breathy, almost exultant with recollection. "They were both dead before they'd gone two steps into the room. The killing was easy. The hard part was setting the scene afterwards. Have you ever tried to undress two dead men? But I did it. I'm a much stronger person now."

"Sure you are. That's why you used me to fetch and carry what you were afraid to go after for yourself."

"Casey . . ." Ford sounded hurt. "I was all alone. I was caught in a squeeze between two very hostile forces: a thug on the one hand, who thought he had a right to half my fortune . . . a gang of scavengers on the other, who wanted it all. Anyway . . . I planned your part in it long before I killed them."

"Suppose I hadn't taken the bait?"

"Then I might have had to risk my own skin. Or I might just have given it all up as a lost cause. But you took the bait. I knew I could count on you. You're so damned inquisitive. And you're a born mother. You should have had a child years ago. Anyway, it all worked out beautifully. Just the way I planned it."

"Not so beautifully, Charles," she said bitterly. "Not quite the ending you planned. Someone got to that vault before I did. There was nothing there but a plastic bag packed with seeds."

Ford took the news with surprising equanimity. "Let me see it, please."

"Why would you think I even bothered to bring it?"

"I know you, Casey. You don't like to leave questions unanswered. If it's not here, it's in your room in Amsterdam." He reached inside his coat and casually drew out a small nickle-plated automatic. "Now, where is it, Casey?" he asked in a voice as cold as death.

LYING ON HIS SIDE on the embankment on the far side of the Volkswagen, Corning searched his pockets until he found his box of matches. With fingers numb and clumsy from the cold, he laboriously unscrewed the valve cap on the car's rear tire. He fumbled a matchstick out of the little box and was about to jam it in against the valve pin when a thought occurred to him. Why immobilize both cars? This one might serve him very well . . . if.

He scrambled along the embankment toward the front of the car. He reached up and opened the door a crack and peered inside. The steering wheel thrust out almost directly above his head. And under the steering wheel he found what he had hoped would be there, the keys dangling from the ignition. He removed the keys and slipped them into his pocket. He closed the door again, but not tightly enough for the latch to engage. Then he searched around on the embankment until he found a fist-sized rock. Now, when the little man returned to the Volkswagen, Corning would be ready.

The man would enter the VW, as he had left it, from the roadside door. He would slide in behind the steering wheel and reach for the keys. Finding them gone, he would instinctively search his pockets. He would be off his guard, with his hands trapped inside his clothes. And that was when Corning would move, jerking the door open, startling the occupant. One sharp blow to the head with the rock and it would be over. Then he would deal with Mrs. Ford.

CASEY LOOKED UNEASILY at the pistol aimed at her middle and said, placatingly, "Charles, I want you to understand. It's not what you may have expected. It's just a plastic bag filled with seeds."

*** **188**

"Let's see it, Casey."

Casey shrugged and reached out to open the glove compartment.

"Wait!" Ford snapped. He had raised the pistol and was pointing it at her head now. "Open that glove compartment very carefully. And remember—if there's a weapon in there you'll have to take hold of it and aim it, and you won't have time for that."

Casey felt tears welling in her eyes. "You're pathetic, Charles. You really are. There's nothing in there worth killing anybody for . . . not even by your set of values." She pressed the release button. The door to the glove compartment fell open. She reached in carefully with both hands and withdrew the plastic bag, blinking back tears.

Ford held out his free hand and took the bag and set it in his lap, kneading it lovingly with his fingers as if it were alive. He seemed more at ease now, almost at peace with himself, like a thirsting man who has found his oasis. He still held the gun pointed at her, but almost casually, the tenseness gone from his fingers. "I wish I could invite you to share this with me," he said. "But I don't think I could trust you. Your scruples would get in the way."

"Share what, Charles? You don't know what's in the bag."

"Of course I do," he said complacently. "Seeds. Hybrid chrysanthemum. *Estrella Azul*. Blue star in Spanish. It's really quite extraordinary, A blossom like a star sapphire. A cream-white iris shooting rays of white across a field of azure petals. The first blue-petaled chrysanthemum ever achieved. The seeds of this first crop are worth almost ten times per ounce their weight in gold."

Casey stared at him as if he were mad.

"You don't understand, do you?" he said contemptuously.

189 ***

"Horticulture is an industry, just like autos or steel or clothing. In some countries, like Holland here, discovering a new blossom is something like tapping a virgin oil field.

"A few years ago I met a man in Rome . . . but you met him too. He was a dilettante botanist. He told me about a man in Cuba who had been working for years on a new strain of chrysanthemum. It was really a sideline with him, an avocation. Cane production was his specialty. Neither the climate nor the soil of his country was conducive to mass-producing the flowers. But he developed it in one of his greenhouses as a labor of love. He had something I wanted. Something easily portable and convertible to cash. I had something he wanted . . . or rather something his country wanted. I had gold. We arranged for an exchange of assets. I established a contact here with a grower who would pay me thirty-five hundred dollars an ounce for that first crop of hybrid seeds. All I need do now is make delivery and leave." With his free hand, Ford began turning the steering wheel of the car.

"Is that where we're going now?" Casey asked, looking past him, hoping to see Corning somewhere outside the car. But the side windows were steamed over and opaque.

"That's where *I'm* going. I'm afraid I'll have to leave you here. We married for better or for worse, Casey; you'll just have to settle for the worse." He kept turning the steering wheel until it would turn no more. "I'm told," Ford said, "that a car having rolled into the water with its windows shut will form an air bubble inside. You may live for a little while. Or would you rather I opened the window and let the end come quickly? I think perhaps I'd better open the window."

Casey closed her eyes and silently prayed that Albert Corning would make his move.

*** **190**

PEERING OUT FROM UNDER THE CHASSIS of the Volkswagen, Corning saw the wheels of the Chrysler begin to turn, heard the engine come alive with a cough. The bastards, he thought as he scrambled up the slope. They've made a deal. Blind with rage, he bolted out from behind the Volkswagen and across the road.

Ford backed the car up a few yards and swung the steering wheel again until the front end was aimed directly seaward. Then, with the engine purring flawlessly he held his foot down on the brake and moved the automatic shift lever from "reverse" to "drive." Through all this he held his pistol pointed directly at Casey's face. "Goodbye, love," he said and took hold of his door handle . . .

. . . as Corning wrenched the door open from the outside. Ford was dragged halfway out of the car by the force of the movement. He lay sideways in the doorway, his foot no longer exerting pressure on the brake. The Chrysler began slowly to roll forward toward the embankment. Casey threw herself across the seat and thrust her hand down on the brake as Corning pulled Ford out onto the road.

The pistol discharged once, as Ford's hand tensed against the trigger, sending a slug cracking over Casey's head and ripping out through the roof of the car. Ford writhed, twisting his body to see who his attacker was as he came sprawling out onto the icy concrete. His eyes went wide with terror and recognition, his mouth gaped in an aborted scream as he tried to bring the pistol up into firing position before Corning's rock came crashing down onto the side of his head.

Ford lay on his back on the road, his feet still trapped within the car. The bag of seeds lay on the road beside him. Corning pried the pistol out of Ford's hand and pulled him the rest of the way out of the car so that he lay stretched out flat.

Casey worked her way across the front seat, maintaining pressure on the foot brake with her right hand while she reached out with her left hand for the parking brake under the dashboard near the door. She pressed down hard, let go of the footbrake, and eased her way out of the car.

She got out onto the road, looked down at Ford and turned away, overcome with a wave of nausea.

"Is he alive?" she asked weakly.

"He's alive," Corning said flatly.

"We've got to get him to a doctor." Casey forced herself to turn back to the body on the road. The concavity in the skull was turning blue. She knelt down beside him to make sure he was still breathing.

"Where the hell were you going with him in the car?"

"Nowhere." She placed her fingers on Ford's neck under his jaw, feeling for a pulse.

"Very neat, indeed. Mr. and Mrs. Ford drive off to pick up their treasure, leaving poor Corning clinging to the dike. Mr. and Mrs. Ford . . . working together 'til death do them part."

"Death was going to part us right here," Casey said. "He meant to leave me locked inside the car and roll it down into the sea. And his money isn't hidden anywhere. It's all right there in the package of seeds."

Corning knelt down, picked up the plastic bag and looked at Casey distrustfully.

"They're a newly developed hybrid. Flowers are big business in Amsterdam, as well as diamonds. There must be over a quarter of a million dollars' worth of seeds in that little package. Now, please, won't you help me with him?"

"I'm afraid not."

*** **192**

Casey looked up at him incredulously. "What kind of man are you? You have your precious treasure. Let the law take care of him. This insane business of retribution can't go on forever."

"I'm afraid I'm not the man you think I am, Mrs. Ford."

Casey rose slowly, staring into the muzzle of the pistol that Corning now held leveled at her. "You see, that story I told you about Charles Ford . . . and his 'partner' . . . and the agents who had been pursuing him . . ."

"It was all a lie," she said with sickening comprehension.

"No. It was all quite true. Except that the roles were reversed. Your friend Rawlings was the agent. And *I* am Charles' unwelcome 'partner.' Now, if you'll get back into the car . . ."

Casey backed away from the gun, into the car. Numbly she sat behind the steering wheel, jumbled thoughts tumbling kaleidoscopically in her head. She remembered the note from A. Wernicke. Eric had not been trying to trick her; he had been trying to save her. He *was* ill, or injured. But his concern for her welfare had been abiding. Regretfully she thought of the apology she owed him and would never be able to deliver. Her only consolation lay in the knowledge that Eric was alive. And she knew that, one day, he would bring Corning down.

"All the way over," Corning ordered. "We don't want to leave Charles lying out here on the road."

Casey slid across the seat. Corning grabbed Ford by the coat collar and roughly hoisted him with one hand into a sitting position.

"For God's sake!" Casey shouted, and started to move across the seat again.

"Back!" Corning ordered, still holding Ford with one hand and pointing the gun with the other. Casey froze.

193 ***

"Be careful with him, please," Casey pleaded.

Corning tucked the bag of seeds inside his coat, half knelt, reached across Ford's chest with his free arm, and hauled him upright. Then he dumped him like a sack into the driver's seat. Ford's head banged against the roof and his body slumped grotesquely in the doorway.

Casey gasped and moved protectively toward him.

"Back!" Corning ordered again, jamming his knee against Ford to keep him from toppling out. Corning straightened him up and packed him like baggage in behind the wheel. He slumped over the wheel and the horn began to blow. Corning shoved him back against the seat.

"You'll kill him," Casey yelled.

"Damned right I will," Corning said.

Corning slammed the door shut on the driver's side of the Chrysler. Holding the pistol in his left hand aimed at Casey, he reached down into the car through the open window and felt around under the dashboard with his right hand until he located the emergency brake. He squeezed the handle until he felt the brake unlock and then he eased it down. With the restraint of the brake gone and the transmission in "drive," the car began to inch forward of its own accord.

The Chrysler's left rear wheel bounced over the cast-off rock that Corning had used as a weapon. The car gave a little lurch. Ford's body slumped sideways against Corning's arm, trapping his hand down below the steering wheel, pulling him off balance. As he tried to free his arm, his elbow brushed the control button for the windows.

Suddenly he was running with the accelerating car, desperately fighting to keep from being dragged, his hand still pinioned by Ford's knee, the window rolling inexorably upward.

*** **194**

Casey saw the panic in his eyes. The gun was no longer aimed at her. She pulled frantically at the handle of her door. It wouldn't budge. The Chrysler was no more than ten feet from the lip of the dike. She remembered the safety catch on her door and released it. At the same moment Corning managed to move Ford's body. The thought flashed through Casey's mind that, even should she get out, Corning would shoot her on the embankment.

The front wheels of the car bounced and dipped over the edge of the embankment. Ford's body fell forward against the wheel again, and again the horn began to blow. Casey felt her door give way. She braced her feet against the hump of the drive-shaft housing and hurled herself out. Tumbling and rolling down the embankment, she heard Corning scream.

The window clamped shut on Corning's forearm just below the elbow. Still running with the car, he managed to slide his arm out to the wrist, the window closing tighter as his arm moved out, finally locking his mammoth hand impassably inside. He tried once to swing at the glass with the gun in his free hand, but by then the car was plunging, pulling him off his feet, breaking his forearm at the wrist, dragging him, howling, along until with a final bounce the Chrysler leapt out over the water, hung poised for a moment, Casey's door flapping open like a broken wing, and then nosedived in.

Near the bottom of the embankment, Casey rose on bloodied knees and watched, helpless and horrified, as the Chrysler rapidly filled and sank out of sight.

Bubbles began rising to the surface, briefly marking the spot where the car had gone down, a boiling cauldron of bubbles at first, and then just a few. And then just one, breaking in a frothy ring at the surface. And then no more.

195 *

She sat dazed on the embankment for a while, unmindful of the cold or the pain in her lacerated knees.

Halfway up the embankment she found the plastic bag. It was trapped in an outcropping of brush, a sad, torn rag of a thing whipping in the wind. It had dropped from under Corning's coat as he struggled to free himself. It had burst open like a great ripe seed pod, its treasure blown and scattered by the gusts coming in off the sea.

She picked up the tattered remnant and found a few of the seeds still caught in an unbroken corner of the bag. She held them between her fingers for a while and then opened her fingers and let the wind take them away. She hoped they would come to rest somewhere on the fertile *poulder*. She hoped they would survive the cold of winter and that something beautiful would grow in the spring.

163